Crocodiles and Rivers

NOVELS FOR ADULT LEARNERS

CROCODILES AND RIVERS

DON SAWYER

CENTRE FOR CURRICULUM, TRANSFER AND TECHNOLOGY
VICTORIA, BRITISH COLUMBIA

Crocodiles and Rivers
by Don Sawyer

This novel has been written especially for adults learners improving their reading skills. The development and production was funded by the Province of British Columbia, Ministry of Education, Skills and Training and Human Resources Development Canada, National Literacy Secretariat.

Project coordination: Centre for Curriculum, Transfer and Technology
Design and production coordination: Bendall Books
Cover design and illustration: Bernadette Boyle

Canadian Cataloguing in Publication Data

Sawyer, Don.
Crocodiles and rivers
(Novels for adult learners)
ISBN 0-7718-9492-9
1. High interest-low vocabulary books. 2. Readers (Adult) I. Centre for Curriculum, Transfer and Technology. II. Title. III. Series.
PS8587.A3C76 1997 428'.62 C97-960066-9
PR9199.3S3C76 1997

NOVELS FOR ADULT LEARNERS	**ORDER NO.**	**ISBN**
The Buckle by Don Sawyer	VA0190	0-7718-9493-7
Crocodiles and Rivers by Don Sawyer	VA0191	0-7718-9492-9
Frozen Tears by Don Sawyer	VA0192	0-7718-9491-0
The Mailbox by Kate Ferris	VA0193	0-7718-9488-0
The Scowling Frog by Kate Ferris	VA0194	0-7718-9490-2
Three Wise Men by Kate Ferris	VA0195	0-7718-9489-9
Package of 6 Novels	CPUB130M	0-7719-1757-0
Activities Handbook for Instructors	VA0276	0-7718-9557-7

ORDERING

Queen's Printer
Government Publication Services
563 Superior Street
PO Box 9452 Stn Prov Govt
Victoria, British Columbia
Canada V8W 9V7

Telephone: 250-356-2820 or 1-888-883-4766
Fax: 250-387-1120
Email: QPPublications@gems5.gov.bc.ca
Web: www.publications.gov.bc.ca

Payment options are by company cheque or money order (no personal cheques) made payable to Minister of Finance; and Visa or Mastercard, including expiry date.

Acknowledgements

I am indebted to travelling companion Wayne Lundeberg for his editorial assistance and advice. I would also like to thank Dr. Eric Nellis of Okanagan University College for his helpful background on the Atlantic slave trade and Bill VanBergyk of the Co-op Mill in Canoe for an orientation to sawmills. I also want to thank George Johnson for sharing his moving personal experiences with me.

Secondary sources for this book include Philip Curtin's *The Atlantic Slave Trade*, C.L.R. James' *The Black Jacobins*, and Mannix and Cowley's *The Middle Passage*. As an historical note, General Maurepas was an actual figure in the Haitian revolution. The character in this book, however, represents a combination of the backgrounds and real experiences of several Haitian generals.

1

A cold March wind blew in from Shuswap Lake. But the men working around the log boom had seen worse. At least it was above freezing.

Ross looked over his shoulder. He was standing on a gangplank that ran in a square around the mill in-feed. The little blue and white boom boat looked like a miniature tug. He watched as it struggled to push another boom of logs to the red Barko. He couldn't see Wayne inside the Barko cab. But he could see the arm of the big machine break the bands holding the logs. It looked kind of like the steam shovel in a kids' book he had read when he was younger. But instead of a bucket at the end of the arm it had almost delicate claws.

Once the logs were freed from the boom they spread out over the water. Terry began to pole them into the lift area toward Ross and Gordy.

"Ross!" Gordy yelled. "Pay attention!"

Ross could hardly hear him over the noise of the Barko, the boom boat and the clanking side lift in front of them. He looked down into the water. Logs had clogged the entrance to the side lift. Gordy was struggling to keep the logs feeding onto the big teeth of the side lift that carried them up to the log deck of the saw mill. Ross stuck his long aluminum pole into the mass of floating logs below. He helped guide a big hemlock onto the teeth and watched it move dripping up the lift. The end of his 16-foot pole had a pointed hook on the end called a pike. He used it to maneuver another log onto the lift.

Ross stamped his feet. The spikes in the bottom of his cork boots dug into the wood gangplank. Geez, it was cold for March. He felt the cold from his pike pole seep through his heavy leather gloves. He took off his yellow hard hat and pulled his white toque down over his ears. It contrasted starkly with the dark skin of his face.

The whistle blew for coffee. The lift stopped and Ross pulled up his pole. He hung it on hooks and walked over toward Gordy. He was standing by the stairs that led up to the yard.

"Man," Gordy complained. "Where were you?"

They walked toward the lunch room.

"I don't know. Just thinking I guess."

Gordy shook his head. "That's always dangerous. Well, think about this. Alan came up while you were dreaming. He said we were to see Walter when our shift is over."

"Walter who?"

"Walter who?" Gordy asked in exasperation. "Walter the mill manager!"

"Oh, *that* Walter."

They pushed the door open to the old lunch room. It was gloriously warm inside. Ross took off his orange insulated vest and hung it on a peg. Yellow rain slickers hung in a line along the wall.

"Yeah, *that* Walter," Gordy continued. "It doesn't look good."

They sat down at the grey table. Aluminum lunch pails and stainless steel coffee thermoses were lined up on both sides.

"Umm." Ross poured steaming coffee into the top of his thermos.

"Great." Gordy sat down and picked up his own thermos. "We're about to be laid off and all you can say is 'Umm.' "

Ross wrapped his hands around the warm cup. "You don't know he's going to lay us off."

"Oh, right. The manager probably just wants to have a little chat with us. Talk things over. Get some advice on how to run the mill. Make sure we're happy with our jobs. Maybe he wants to know about the family."

Other men were filing into the building. They nodded at Ross and Gordy.

"Maybe he does. You don't know."

Now Gordy was irritated. "Come on, Ross. You know what's been going on. They've shut down our burners so we can't burn the chips and sawdust. There is such a glut the paper companies can't handle it. And the government won't give the mill a permit to export. The whole mill is all backed up. They're laying guys off right and left."

"Yeah, well, you're probably right."

Gordy sat back in his chair shaking his head. "We're about

ready to lose our jobs. And you seem about as concerned as if I told you it was expected to drizzle this afternoon! Did you get some money in the mail or something?"

Ross looked up. He smiled oddly.

"No money. But I got something in the mail. Picked it up this morning. A registered package from Haiti."

"Haiti? Why Haiti?"

"I'm not sure. That's where my parents were from, you know."

"Oh yeah. I guess you did tell me. So what's in the package?"

The whistle went to start the last part of the afternoon shift.

"I don't know. I didn't have a chance to open it. I'll look at it tonight."

The two men got up and slipped their vests back on. "You want to go to the Railbird after work?"

The Railbird was the pub nearest the mill. It was a few kilometres away between the railroad tracks and the lake. It looked over a grebe nesting site.

"Yeah, sure. Sounds like a good idea. But let's get the afternoon over."

When the whistle blew to end the afternoon shift, Ross and Gordy hung up their poles. They climbed the metal ladder that led up to the mill itself. They walked by the outside log deck. Manny was the head rig operator. He was still in his glassed cabin putting through the last of the logs. They watched as he punched the buttons on his handles like a giant Nintendo game. The huge logs were placed on the carriage. A red laser beam showed where the first cut would be. Then the logs slid through the saws. They came back white where the first slab had been cut. Then Manny turned them for the next cut.

Gordy opened the door into the mill. They walked into a wall of noise. There was the bumping of logs. The shrieking of saws. Cut lumber clattered along belts below them. Chains clanked everywhere. The men working inside wore ear guards over their hard hats. They looked like grey plastic earmuffs.

Ross and Gordy walked along the metal catwalks. They could see through the grating to the moving lines of timber below. They passed by John, the head sawyer. He sat in another glassed booth. Inside it looked like the cockpit of an airplane. Red and green lights glowed. Lines of switches and buttons arced around John on both sides. Television monitors glowed with pictures of the wood as he adjusted it for the best possible cuts.

"If *he* gets laid off," Gordy shouted, "he can become an airline pilot."

Ross could only make out a few words. He cupped his hand around his ear. "What's that?"

"I said," Gordy began to yell. But the noise was deafening. "Oh, never mind."

"What?"

"Never mind!" Gordy screamed.

"You've lost your mind?"

Gordy thought about strangling him. Then he saw Ross grinning. He laughed.

They walked over the log lines. They heard the scanner sizing up timber and shuttling it into saws. And the steady whine of the band saws.

They waved to Alex, the resaw operator. He was just shutting down. It was quieter now.

"I heard Alex was leaving," Gordy yelled.

Ross nodded.

"I think I'll bid on his job."

"You want to work in here?" Ross asked. "It's a madhouse!"

"It's better than freezing your ass off outside feeding that damned side lift."

Ross shook his head. "Not for me. I'll take cold and relative quiet any day."

They finally got to the mill manager's office. It was at the back of the building. A huge pane of glass opened up on the mill. They could see Walter sitting behind his desk. Paper was stacked in a pile on both sides of his dark green blotter. They walked to the door and knocked.

Walter never looked up. "Come in."

They opened the door and walked in. As the heavy metal door closed there was near silence.

Walter finally finished filling in numbers on the sheet in front of him. He pushed the paper away and sat back in his maroon chair. He put his pen in a cup on the desk and looked at Gordy and Ross.

"Geez, I hate paper work. Seven years as a manager and I still can't get used to it." He sighed. "Anyway, that's not why I called you in." Walter paused. Gordy looked at the job board on the wall.

Each job had a magnetized name stuck under it. There were about 50 name tags clustered on one side under "Laid off." He noticed that his and Ross's names were still under "Log Lift Helper." He wondered how long they would stay there.

"You men have done very well here," Walter was saying. "You've worked hard and done a good job. And that's what makes this so much harder." He ran his fingers though his thin grey hair.

"But as you know, we've had trouble moving our chips. We're down to a skeleton crew. Guys with seniority are bumping all over the place. We're going to have to lay the two of you off for a while. Just a while, I hope. Until we can get this glut of chips sorted out."

Gordy nodded. "Yeah, we kind of figured that was what was coming. When are we done?"

"End of next week." Walter shrugged his shoulders. "That's the best I can do. Sorry."

Now Ross spoke. "How long do you think we'll be laid off?"

"Not long, I hope. Two, three months. Something's got to give soon."

"Two or three months, eh?" Gordy sighed. "It's not easy living on UI."

Walter shook his head. "I know, I know. I really hate being manager at times like this. But what can I do?"

Ross leaned against the window. He glanced at the chain of yellow teeth carrying cut lumber to the sorting bins.

"Well, I guess that's it. Thanks for talking to us."

Walter stood up. "Good luck."

The mill was almost quiet as they walked back over the catwalks.

"You want a ride to the Railbird?" Ross asked as they clambered down the stairs. They walked toward the tracks and the parking lot on the other side.

"Nah," Gordy replied. "I'll drive over. I need a minute to process this. See you over there."

2

The Railbird tried to look like an English pub. There was lots of oak veneer on the walls. A big wood bar curved across one side. Old British newspapers declaring the end of World War II and Churchill's resignation hung on the wall. The wood tables and chairs were dark and heavy. But somehow it didn't quite make it. TV sets glowed in every corner. The Vancouver Canucks were playing Calgary. A bunch of guys leaned on pool cues around a big pool table in a corner. The main floor of the pub was filled with tables. A gaudy chandelier hung from the high ceiling. The place was too big, too loud and too open to be cozy.

Ross and Gordy headed for an empty table near the rear door. They maneuvered through the tables crowded with beer glasses and laughing drinkers.

"Boy, I'll never get used to it," Ross muttered as they sat down.

"What's that?"

"I'll never get used to being stared at every time I walk into a place."

"Ah, you're just too sensitive."

"You think so?"

"Yeah. They're not staring. And if they are they're just curious. They don't mean anything. After all, you are black."

"Thanks for pointing that out."

"Come on. You know what I mean. You just don't see many black guys around here."

Ross sat down and stared at the shiny wood table top. "I'm tired of being a curiosity. Exotic. Like some kind of rare animal at a zoo."

Gordy pulled out the chair opposite Ross. He sat down and leaned back. He shook his head. "You're making too much of it."

Ross looked up sharply.

"Oh yeah? And how many times have you been stopped by the cops when you leave the pub?"

Gordy shrugged. "Never."

"I've been stopped 14 times. Fourteen! The cops say they just want to make sure I'm not a danger. And one time I was with Pete. I was giving him a lift back to his truck."

"Yeah."

"So they stopped me, as usual. Now you know me. I hardly drink. I'd had one beer. And Pete had drunk about four. He was half cut. But you know what they did? They insisted that Pete drive. They made me get out of the car and let Pete drive! Was that just coincidence."

"Could be."

"Could be, yeah. And how many times have you been stopped while driving with your girlfriend?"

"Well, once or twice when I was speeding."

"Yeah, well Allison and I have been stopped at least six times. They ask to look at my registration. Where I'm going. And in Vancouver they made me get out of the car and spread on the hood. I wasn't doing anything. Frisked me. Asked me if I was carrying drugs. If I was a pimp. Do you think having a white woman in the front seat with me might have had something to do with it?"

Gordy scowled uncomfortably. "Well, you don't know..."

"OK, I'll give you a few more examples. When I first moved into my place over on Okanagan, I had Shorty, my little dog."

"Yeah, I remember him."

"So I used to take him for a walk every day. Broad daylight. For the first six days the cops stopped me. Six straight days! I was just walking along the sidewalk and they'd pull up. They asked for ID. Asked me what I was doing. That sort of thing."

"Well, why'd they do that?"

"Exactly. So I finally asked them. The neighbours had called. Said there was a suspicious man in the area. And why was I suspicious? Huh?"

Ross kept his voice low, but his usually soft eyes had become hard. He leaned across the table toward Gordy.

"And you know, half the time they don't know they're being racist. Hell, maybe they're not. You have to be aware to be racist. These guys just assume you're black, you're dangerous, you're poor."

"You're poor?"

Ross gave a short laugh and sat back. "Yeah. Listen to this. It's true, I swear it. I was downtown with Allison. It was Christmas time. She had just run into the bank to get out some money. So I was standing outside waiting for her. Just standing there. And this guy walks up. 'Tough times, eh?' he says to me. I don't know what he's getting at. So I say, 'Yeah. Tough times.' Well the guy fishes out his wallet and pulls out a five. He gives it to me. Then he says, 'Here's something to help hold you over.' Now what was that all about? I'm probably making more than this guy, but he assumes I'm down and out."

Gordy laughed. "Maybe you had that ratty jean jacket on. Did you keep the money?"

"Damned right," Ross grinned.

Just then a guy that worked at the mill walked by the table. He ran a forklift in the yard. He was a burly guy with a Blue Jays baseball cap on backwards.

"Hey, Gordy," he said, extending his hand. "How are you doing? Mind if I sit down?"

"Sure." Gordy motioned to an empty chair. "Ross, this is Lawrence Packard. Lawrence, Ross Maurepas."

Ross nodded. "Lawrence."

"Hey, haven't you guys got any beer yet?" Lawrence asked. He raised his hand. "Peggy!" he shouted. A waitress busy at another table looked up. "Three drafts over here!"

He turned back to the table. He looked at Ross. "So how long have you been at the mill?"

"About a year and a half."

"Really? Funny we haven't met. Where you from?"

Ross looked at his hands on the table. “Quebec.”

“Sure, sure, but where are you *really* from. You know what I mean.”

Ross looked up into Lawrence’s smiling face. There was a flickering in Ross’s eyes that made Gordy nervous.

“Where are you *really* from?” Ross asked softly.

Lawrence looked puzzled. “What do you mean? I’m a true blue Canadian. I was born here!”

“So was I,” Ross said quietly.

“Yeah, well...” Lawrence blustered uncertainly.

“Hey, Lawrence,” Gordy broke in. “What do you think about the chip situation?”

Lawrence looked at Gordy, relieved. “Bad situation,” he said. “Bad. Look, I’m sitting with a few guys over here. I gotta get back.” He motioned vaguely with his head. “Nice seeing you guys.” He nodded to Ross and stood up.

“Man,” Gordy said after Lawrence had left. “Why’d you give him such a hard time? He didn’t mean anything.”

Ross sighed. “None of them mean anything. None of them. But I’m tired of it, Gordy. Tired of dealing with it every day. It takes different forms, but it’s always there.”

The waitress brought them their beers.

“Oh, I thought there were three of you.”

“There were,” Gordy said. “But just leave the third beer. I need it.”

3

"You know that package I told you I got yesterday in the mail?"

It was noon. Ross and Gordy were at the end of the table in the lunch room. There were no lights on. The low clouds outside made the room grey and gloomy.

Gordy looked up from his sandwich. "You mean the one from Haiti?"

Ross nodded. "Yeah. Well I opened it last night. Pretty interesting."

Ross sipped coffee from the top of his thermos and looked out a window over Gordy's shoulder.

"Yeah?" Gordy said finally in exasperation. "Go on."

"What?"

"Jesus, Ross. You started telling me about this package and then you faded off into the ozone."

Ross put his coffee down. He folded his hands on the table.

"Sorry. Well, it was pretty interesting."

"You already said that. What was interesting about it?"

"Well, they were copies of some old papers."

"Nuts," Gordy muttered. "I was hoping you'd inherited a plantation in Haiti and you and I had to go down there and claim it."

Ross smiled. "Not quite. There was a letter with the package. It was from a Dr. Mary Wilson. She's from Yale or Georgetown or some university in the U.S. Anyway, she's doing research on the Haitian revolution. You know much about it?"

Gordy shook his head. "I didn't even know they *had* a revolution."

"Well they did. After the U.S., the first successful revolt by a colony. And it was carried out by slaves. It created the first independent state in the Caribbean. Started in 1791."

"So what's this got to do with your package?"

"Well, I knew I had an ancestor that fought with Toussaint l'Ouverture." Ross said. Gordy's face was blank. "He was the slave that led the revolt. Anyway, my ancestor's name was Michel Maurepas."

"Same last name as yours."

"Yeah. He was a general with l'Ouverture. And for one wonderful year there was peace. During that year, 1801, he was a governor of a district. Anyway, after things broke down the French put him under house arrest. They arrested Toussaint l'Ouverture too. Sent him back to France. He died there in prison."

"Thanks for the history lesson. But I still don't see what this has to do with the papers."

"Well this woman..."

"Dr. Mary Wilson."

"Right, Dr. Wilson. She was looking for old documents relating to the revolution. She visited people in Haiti connected to revolutionary figures. She found this family in Cap François. An ancestor of theirs had worked for General Maurepas. As a secretary or something. They had a package they had kept in their family for 200 years. It was General Maurepas' story. He dictated it while under arrest. Then he gave it to his secretary to keep safe."

Gordy had forgotten the lunch in front of him. "Wow! So the package you got were these papers."

"Right. Well copies of them. She has a copy. The family got a copy. She got the family to let her put the original in a library in Haiti."

"Amazing. After 200 years. How'd she find you?"

"Well, she tried to find the descendants of Maurepas. She traced them to my parents in Montreal. Then she found out they had died. So she went through the records and got my name. She traced me through family back in Quebec. I guess I am the last direct descendant."

"So what do the papers say?"

"I haven't gotten through them all yet. They're handwritten, of course. And the French is a real old style."

"You speak French?"

"Mais oui. Bien sur."

"What's that mean?"

"It means 'Of course I do, you dummy.' "

Just then the whistle went for the afternoon shift. Gordy hurriedly stuffed his sandwich in his mouth. He tilted the thermos up to wash the baloney sandwich down.

"Yow!" he yelled as the hot liquid burned his lips. He put his thermos back in his lunch box. "By the way, what happened to Maurepas? You know, the general."

Ross clicked his shiny aluminum lunch pail shut. "The French killed him. But first they stripped him naked. Then they nailed epaulettes onto his shoulders."

"They *nailed* them?"

"Then they drowned his entire family in front of him."

"Jesus. What about you? I mean, if they killed his family, how did you get here?"

"He had one son who was fighting with another general. He survived. He was my great-great-about-six-times grandfather."

The two men slipped on their bright orange vests.

"So what have you read so far?" Ross asked.

"I'll tell you more later. After I've gotten into it more. But what's really interesting is that he tells his story beginning in Africa."

"You're kidding. He was born in Africa?"

"Yeah. There were about 500,000 slaves in Haiti in 1791. About two-thirds had been born in Africa."

"So he tells about the whole experience? Being shipped from Africa and everything?"

"Yeah. That's what they called the middle passage. I've gotten through that pretty well. But we better get going. I'll tell you more after work."

4

"OK, so let me get this straight." Ross and Gordy were at the Railbird two days later. Gordy picked up his clear glass mug and finished the last of his beer. "This guy Maurepas was a chief's son. His tribe were the Mandingue?"

"I guess that's what his tribe was. He wrote that that was his language anyway."

"And what do you know about the Mandingue?"

"Only what he writes. I have to find out more. But he says his people lived by a river. They fished and raised crops. They had many craftsmen. Some worked leather. Others metal. There were special singers, called griots, who told the stories of the community. They were the historians. And they had laws. Sculpture. Sounds like they were doing pretty well."

"So what happened?"

"Well, you know, the Europeans wanted slaves. They killed off all the Indians. So they needed workers for their sugar plantations. They wanted Africans because they were more immune to the diseases in South America and the Caribbean. From what I've read, they sent over 10 million Africans to the New World as slaves."

Gordy whistled. "Ten million!"

"Maybe more. Of course the conditions were so terrible that often 30 percent would die on the way."

"So tell me this guy's story."

"Well, he was captured by a coastal tribe looking for slaves. He was shackled hand and foot. Connected by chains to 35 others. Then he was marched for over 10 days. He tells about a woman and her daughter who passed out from exhaustion. They were abandoned to the wild animals. The slaves were blistered by the sun. And terrified. He wrote that many of them believed they were to be eaten.

"So they were finally carried out to this island. Gore, Gory, something like that. I couldn't quite make it out. Anyway, once they got there they were branded like cattle. Then they were kept in these crowded little cells for months. Finally they were loaded onto canoes to take them to the slave ships. They knew they would never come back. Maurepas wrote that people were whipped and dragged into the canoes. He said that he was behind a canoe going toward a ship. All of a sudden the whole group of slaves jumped out of the boat into the sea. They stayed under water until they drowned. They would rather die than become slaves. And be taken from their land."

"Jesus." Gordy shook his head. "Then what."

"Maybe the worst part of all. They were shipped like animals. Shackled in twos. They were packed on rough wood floors. Maurepas wrote that he had less room than a corpse in a coffin. They were jammed together like spoons in a drawer. The ceilings were too low to even sit up. They got out above board only twice a day. And that was if the weather was good."

"Wait a minute," Gordy said. His eyes were wide. "I need another beer. Want one?"

Ross shook his head. Gordy yelled to the waitress. "Peggy! One more draft." The he looked back at Ross. "That sounds incredible. How long did it take?"

"Maurepas wrote that they had pretty good weather. It only took them six weeks. But some passages took up to three months."

"My God." Gordy's beer arrived. He took a quick sip. "So what else did he say?"

"He said they were brought on deck once in the morning. Their shackles were attached to long chains around the ship's side. They were given boiled rice. Then they were made to dance."

"Dance?"

"Yeah. They had to jump up and down in their chains. They were lashed if they didn't."

"Why on earth would they make them do that?"

"The crews thought it kept the slaves from committing suicide."

"Were there lots of suicides?"

"In his story Maurepas wrote that some of the slaves thought that if they died they would return to their homes. He said that once two men jumped overboard and drowned. Another time a woman found some rope and strangled herself. The captain made the slaves come up on deck. He beheaded the corpse before he threw it overboard. He told them that they would return to their friends headless if they killed themselves. But that did not stop them. According to Maurepas, many starved themselves to death. But the crews had a clamp. They pried the slave's mouth open and poured food into the mouth through a funnel."

"It sounds like hell."

"Yeah, but disease was the worst. In his account he says that some sort of stomach illness broke out among the slaves. There was vomit and diarrhoea everywhere. The holds stunk so bad that he kept gagging. Then there was a storm. They had to keep the slaves below for four days. They shut the ports. The ship pitched and rolled. The skin on some slaves' elbows was worn away to the bone. The stench was overpowering."

Gordy took a deep breath. "My God. How can people do that to other people?"

"It doesn't seem possible, but according to Maurepas, when they got to Haiti things got worse. They were sold. Then they were put in rough barracks and made to work incredibly long hours. They were beaten. Man, some of the cruelties Maurepas writes about are hard to believe."

"Like what?"

"Sometimes slaves were whipped to death. For almost nothing. And salt, pepper and hot ashes would be poured into the bleeding wounds. They'd cut off limbs and ears. The masters would pour burning wax on their arms and shoulders. Poured boiling cane sugar over their heads. Roasted them on slow fires. They filled them up with gunpowder and blew them up. They'd bury slaves up to their necks and smear their heads with sugar. The ants and flies would eat them alive..." Ross's voice trailed off. "There were more."

Gordy rubbed his eyes. "That's enough," he said quietly. "So they revolted."

"Yeah," Ross replied. "And they did a pretty good job of it. First they defeated the colonists. Then the English thought they could take over. But l'Ouverture stopped them. Kicked them right off the island. And there was a short peace. L'Ouverture set up schools. Great buildings were built. A government system was put in place. Farms worked by freed slaves did really well. Things were looking up."

"So what happened?"

"Napoleon."

"Napoleon Bonaparte?"

"That's the one. See, Haiti—they called it San Domingo back then—had been a French colony. They wanted it back. They wanted to restore slavery. They sent 60,000 crack soldiers against a ragtag army of ex-slaves. It was terrible. It went on for almost three years. Everything was destroyed. But finally the blacks won. Of the 60,000 French troops, nearly all had died in battle or from disease. But the place was devastated. The most able leader was dead. Haiti never recovered."

"Jeez, no wonder."

"Yeah. That's why my parents left. Looking for something better."

There was a long silence. Gordy sat back in his chair and sipped his beer. Ross watched a couple of guys playing pool.

"Man, this Maurepas guy's story is pretty heavy," Gordy said at last. "Are you glad you got it?"

Ross turned his empty mug back and forth.

"Oh yeah. A lot of it I knew already. This just makes it more real. More personal. But the most interesting part for me is his writing on Africa. I didn't know anything about that. Where we were from. What tribe we were part of. How we lived. Anything."

"Yeah, that's neat. You going to do anything with it?"

Ross paused thoughtfully. "I don't know. I want to do a little research. Find out more. And then I've got an idea."

"What's that?"

Ross grinned and looked up at his friend. "It's just a wild idea."

5

"Gordy, let's go to Africa," Ross yelled. Gordy stood at the other end of the gangplank poling logs. He cupped his hand over his ear.

"I can hardly hear you. I thought you said, 'Let's go to Africa.' "

There was no wind, but the drone of the Barko made talking difficult.

"I did," Ross yelled back.

"Right," Gordy shouted back. "We're laid off in three more days and you want to go to Africa. Well, I've always been real interested in Saturn. Why don't we go there?"

"No, I'm serious. We can do it."

Gordy shook his head and waved his left hand at Ross. "You're talking crazy. At least I think you are. I can hardly hear you. Wait till lunch."

An hour later, Gordy had his baloney sandwich laid out on wax paper. Ross sat across from him munching on an apple.

"All right," Gordy began. "Now what were you saying out there? Something nutty about going to Africa?"

"It's not nutty. We can do it."

"Listen, Ross. The farthest I've been is Alberta. And you want to go to Africa? That would cost a fortune."

Ross put his apple down. He leaned forward. "How much money you got saved up?"

"I don't know. Maybe three, four thousand. But that wouldn't be enough."

"Yes it would. Way more than enough! I looked into it. Listen, they've got these charter flights to London. They've got to fill the seats. Usually with tour groups. But if there are empty seats they sell them really cheap. Look at this."

Ross pulled a newspaper page out of his lunch pail. He spread it on the table.

"See. Round trip to London, $499."

Gordy studied the page uncertainly. "OK, so we could get to London. But what about Africa?"

"I got that covered too. You know those Maurepas papers?"

Gordy sighed. "I figured it had something to do with those."

"Well, I went up to the college, to the library. The librarian helped me. You remember that Maurepas wrote that he was a Mandingue?"

"Yeah."

"Well, Mandingue is the old name for the Malinke people. They're also called Mandinka or Mandingo. Most live in the Senegambia region."

"Where's that?"

"West Africa. It's two countries now. Senegal and The Gambia."

"So you want to go to this Senegambia. How are you going to get there? Canoe?"

"No, man. Come on. It turns out that The Gambia is a big tourist area. People from England go down for the winter. It's warm. They've got sandy beaches. They've got cheap air fares. Look!"

This time Ross pulled out a glossy brochure. It had pictures of beaches and palm trees. Swimming pools with happy guests lounging around.

"See, this is for The Gambia. Nice, eh?"

"They all speak Mandinka there?"

"No. Gambia was an English colony. So English is the official language. And then they speak seven or eight tribal languages too."

Gordy still shook his head. "I can't afford that."

"Yes you can. The agent I talked to said there is a cheap tour out of London to Gambia. We get air fare and a hotel for two weeks for 600 bucks!"

"Really?" Gordy said dreamily. "Africa, eh?" Then he snapped back. "But what about our Unemployment?"

"I checked into that. We're laid off on Friday. We go in Monday with our papers. We file for benefits. We put down that we're travelling for a month. But look, it takes a month to process our application anyway. So when we get back we go back in. We let them know we're ready for work. And they start our cheques in a couple of weeks."

Gordy shook his head. "Listen, man. I don't know..."

"Look," Ross said. Ross was leaning across the table. Gordy stared at his sandwich in front of him. He played with the wax paper nervously.

"You want to stay here all your life?" Ross went on. "What do you have to lose?"

Gordy didn't look up. "Just about everything I've managed to save up."

"And what are you going to do if you stay? Hang out in the Railbird? Play pool? Watch TV? That sounds real exciting. Come on, Gordy. Here's a chance to see something different. Grow! Take some chances!"

Gordy looked up at Ross. He met Ross's eyes. He smiled a little. "Africa, eh?"

"You sure you got your tickets?" Gordy asked anxiously. They were heading for the Kelowna airport in Ross's pickup. It had been only eight days since Ross had suggested going to Africa. They had just received their rush passports the day before. And now they were leaving.

"Would you quit worrying?" Ross said. "I told you I checked."

Gordy started rummaging through his bag on the floor.

"What are you doing?" Ross asked.

"Just making sure." He pulled out his ticket. Then his passport. "Yep, they're here."

"They should be. That's the sixth time you've looked since we left."

"I just want to be sure."

"Look, just relax. We're on an adventure. It's supposed to be fun."

"How many time zones away is this place?

"I don't know. Seven or eight."

"Jeez. I had trouble adjusting when I went to Calgary. They were just one hour ahead."

Ross laughed.

"And it's 10 hours on the plane to London?"

"Yeah, something like that."

"Man. The only time I flew I went down to Reno. That was about two or three hours. I ate so many peanuts I thought I was going to throw up."

"Yeah, it's a long way. And when we get to London we have to wait five hours for the plane to Gambia. It's going to be a long day."

Gordy was quiet for a while. He stared out the window at the yellow sunflowers along the highway. "I kind of like it here," he said nervously. "You know, this guy Maurepas is turning out to be a pain in the ass."

6

"Man," Ross said. "I can't believe you're doing that." They had gotten off the plane at Gatwick airport an hour before. They had made their way through immigration without any trouble. Now they were in the main terminal. Gordy had found a cafeteria that was open early in the morning.

"Doing what?" Gordy took his tray and set it down on a table.

"You're having a beer at..." Ross looked at his watch. "At 7:30 in the morning."

Gordy's eyes were red. "Who the hell knows what time it is?" he said grumpily. "Sure, it's 7:30 here. But we left at 1:00. We flew for 10½ hours. Packed like sardines in that damned plane. And we've been here for an hour. So it's 12:30 B.C. time. And that's a great time to have a beer. Besides, I have to take my vitamins."

Gordy opened up his gym bag. "Vancouver Grizzlies" was written across one side. The picture of a ferocious bear lunged out from the other side. He found his shaving kit and unzipped it. He took out a large white bottle and poured pills into his hand.

"You're taking vitamins with beer?"

"Yeah. Why not? Beer's good for you."

"Aren't you afraid that stuff will react with the beer and explode in your stomach?"

Gordy took his handful of pills and tossed them into his mouth. He lifted the bottle of beer to his mouth and swallowed.

"Umm. This English beer's not bad. Little flat, but not bad. Want some?"

"Aargh," Ross croaked, sticking out his tongue. "I'll stick with orange juice."

"Suit yourself. But I'm going to have a couple more of these and try to get some sleep. I feel like someone poured sand in my eyes."

Ross took a sip of his orange juice. "You didn't sleep on the plane?"

"Sleep? I could hardly breathe. I was in the middle seat, remember? *You* had the aisle seat."

"Now, now. Don't be a bad loser. It was just luck."

"Yeah, well, anyway the guy next to me kept kicking me. Then he'd be asleep and his head would fall onto my shoulder. Never even woke up! Plus he snored."

"I'm sure it wasn't that bad."

"How would you know? You were asleep the moment we left Vancouver. How can you do that?"

"I don't know. I've always been that way. I can sleep anytime, anywhere. But look." Ross spread his arms. "Here we are. We're in London!"

Gordy looked around. "Could have fooled me. It looks like a bigger version of the Calgary airport to me."

"Ah, true. But here's the point—it *isn't.* Next stop, my friend, is Africa!"

The plane dropped out of the clouds approaching the Banjul airport. Ross's face was pressed against the window. Gordy was leaning across the seat peering over Ross's shoulder. Suddenly below them they saw the runway. All around was dry scrub land. Palm trees spread out like green dots.

"Mother Africa," Ross said quietly.

"For you, maybe," Gordy mumbled.

"Huh?" Ross turned slightly. "Oh, I was just thinking aloud. But you know, there's one theory that all humans had a common ancestor. The mother of mankind. Eve, they nicknamed her. Two million years ago. And she lived in Africa." He turned back to the window. "So if they're right, we all started here."

Gordy looked down with even more interest. Their plane swung low and approached the landing strip. The wheels touched down. They were in Africa.

Africa hit them from the moment they walked out of the plane. The heat struck first. Then from the top of the stairs they could see the dry, unfamiliar country stretch out on all sides.

Gordy and Ross followed the rest of the passengers across the tarmac. They passed through a fence and then walked toward the entrance into the terminal. A thin black and white cat watched from underneath a plastic table as they walked by.

Inside, long lines formed. People pushed and shoved to get through immigration. Gordy and Ross were separated. Gordy felt the sweat roll down his forehead as he waited. By the time he finally got to the booth, his shirt was soaked. A man in a pale green shirt and darker green beret sat at a wood counter. Gordy gave him his passport.

"You're from Canada?" the man asked.

"That's right," Gordy answered proudly.

"How long will you be staying in The Gambia?"

"Uh, let me see." Gordy spotted Ross in the line next to him. "Ross," he yelled. "How long are we staying?"

"Twenty-four days," Ross shouted back.

"Right." Gordy looked at the immigration officer. "Twenty-four."

The man stamped his passport and wrote something in pen. "Go ahead."

When Gordy stepped away he walked into sheer bedlam. Passengers crushed up against a low fence. Tractors pulling wagons loaded with baggage pulled up. Men unloaded the bags. Other men in grey jackets put them in lines. People were shouting. Ross walked up to Gordy and stood beside him.

"Get through OK?" he asked.

"Yeah, fine. Ross, you notice anything?"

"You mean how dry it is?"

"No, I mean how everybody is black."

Ross laughed hard. "Well, Gordy, old buddy. Welcome to Africa." Just then the gate in the fence was opened. People rushed forward to get their bags. Three men in grey coats ran up to Gordy. One got to him first.

"Which are your bags, sir?"

People were scurrying. They were grabbing bags and heading for the exit. He wasn't sure what the guy wanted. But he wanted to find his bags, too. Fast. He pushed through the other passengers. Gordy finally spotted his old brown suitcase, and started for it. The man who had approached him ran up and grabbed the bag. "Follow me," he said.

Gordy did as he was told. The man carried the bag to a table. A customs official marked an "X" on it with chalk. The porter carried the bag through another gate. They were outside the airport.

Ross walked up. "Let's get a cab."

The porter was already dragging Gordy's bag to an old white Peugeot. "Right over here, sirs."

Ross and Gordy walked over. The driver was already opening up the trunk.

"How much to the Bungalow Beach Hotel?" Ross asked.

"One hundred and twenty dalassis."

"What's a dalassi?" Gordy muttered.

"That's their money. It's about eight to the Canadian dollar, I think."

"That's 15 bucks!"

Ross turned back to the driver. "Nah, I think we'll try to find another way in." He picked up his bag.

"All right, sir," the driver said hurriedly. "You are my friends. Eighty dalassis."

Ross put his bag back down. He looked at Gordy. "What do you think?"

"Listen, man. I'm tired. Let's go for it."

Ross threw his bag in the open trunk. "OK."

The porter tossed Gordy's suitcase in. Then he waited impatiently.

"I think he wants a tip, Gordy."

Gordy pulled a handful of coins out of his pocket. "I sure don't have any of those, what'd you call them? Dalassis?"

"Give him some English money."

Gordy took a pound coin and gave it to the man. His hand folded over the coin. "Thank you, sir!" he said. "Have a good stay in The Gambia."

Ross and Gordy got in the car. "Well," Ross said. "I guess you made that guy's day."

"What do you mean?"

"The average income here is about $350 a year. You just gave that guy two bucks."

The cab was racing down a long drive. The trunks of the trees planted on each side were painted white. Soon they came to the main road. The driver turned right. The road was paved but narrow. Holes gaped every few feet. The driver seemed to ignore all but the largest. The car slammed through them as he sped along the highway.

It was dusk now. The sky was a deep pink. As they drove it gave way suddenly to darkness.

"Man," Gordy marvelled. "Did you notice that? One minute it

was light. And then it was dark. Just like a curtain had been pulled down."

Ross smiled. "Yep. That's nightfall in the tropics."

Along the route rough tables were piled with fruit. Kerosene lanterns were lit beside them or hanging in trees. Families gathered in the circle of light. Some were cooking over a gas stove. Mothers lay against the trunks of the trees holding babies. Soon a low line of shops appeared on each side of the road. People milled along the shoulders of the highway. Women carrying large enamelled bowls and baskets on their heads were lit by the headlights. Many were wearing colourful loose dresses.

The shops had metal roofs and were lit from inside. Handmade beds and chairs were being sold in one place. A man repairing tires was working in another. Music blared from a low cement block building called "The Hollywood Club." More and more people crowded the road. A huge bus roared at them coming the other way. Gordy closed his eyes. But somehow the driver got by without colliding.

Gordy could smell wood smoke and diesel exhaust through the open windows. The noise of people talking filled the night. The cab rushed by a cart being pulled by a scrawny donkey. Two goats stood and looked at them curiously.

The shops were crowded more densely. Side roads appeared lined with more stores. Hundreds of people walked slowly along the roads. Cars wove through the pedestrians and goats.

"Serekunda," the driver said from the front.

"What's that?" Gordy asked.

"This is Serekunda. Big town."

The cab had been slowed by the crowds of people on the road. They flowed by and around the traffic. Many of the men wore long robes that snapped up the front. Most were richly embroidered. They were yellow, lavender, red. Some of the men wore white caps that fit closely on their heads. The women were wrapped in the colourful printed cloth they had seen earlier. A lot of them wore matching turbans. The sounds, smells and people closed around them.

"Jesus," Gordy said softly to Ross. "Where are we?"

The cab threaded its way through the crowd. The road became four lanes. The people and buildings thinned. They came to an intersection. The driver turned left. They made their way through the night. Finally the driver pulled into a brightly lit area. There were several hotels. He drove through a gate in a white wall. An elephant and "Bungalow Beach" were painted on the wall. Inside he pulled up to a building and stopped. There was a long porch across the front.

The driver opened up the trunk and pulled out the bags.

"I'll go inside and change some money so we can pay him," Ross said. He disappeared into the office. Gordy stood in the quiet. He could hear frogs chirping. And from a distance he heard the low crashing of waves on a beach. The stars stood out more brightly than he had ever remembered seeing them.

Ross returned. He gave the driver some bills. The cab pulled away.

"I got our key," Ross said. Gordy kept staring up at the sky. "You all right?"

"Huh? Oh, yeah," Gordy said. "Just tired."

They walked down the long rows of white buildings. The surf became louder. Ross led Gordy up a flight of stairs. They went along a balcony past several darkened rooms. Near the end Ross stopped. He opened a door with a key. He flicked on a light. There was a main room with a small kitchenette, a table and a couch. In the next room there were two beds. Louvered glass windows opened onto the warm night.

Gordy dropped his bag inside and went back on the long balcony outside their room. He sat on one of the chairs. He listened to the waves. In the courtyard a tall coconut palm loomed higher than the porch. Gordy heard the palm fronds rustle in the breeze off the sea.

Ross came out with a glass of water. He sat in the chair across from Gordy.

"Well, what do you think?"

Gordy smiled in the darkness. "Well, Ross, one thing's for sure. This certainly isn't Canada."

The night was warm. The waves rumbled in the background.

"Ross," Gordy said. "Tell me something."

"Sure."

"Why are we here?"

In the darkness Gordy could see Ross roll the empty glass between his hands.

"What do you mean?" Ross asked.

"I mean this is exciting, real exciting. I'm grateful you pried me out of Canada. Whatever happens, this is the greatest adventure of my life. But there's something more going on. For me, this is an exotic vacation. For you it's something more."

Ross sat back heavily in the plastic chair. His left arm lay across the table. He stared over the railing into the African night.

"I don't know exactly." Ross's voice was low, almost a whisper. "All my life I've felt like an outsider. I was always looking for… I don't know."

"How about Haiti?"

"Nah. I went there a few times. But it didn't feel right. I couldn't relate."

"So this is kind of like that book. What was it called? *Roots*?"

"Nah. It's not like that. That was fiction. The guy made it up. He had his character travel from America and find his long-lost village. His family. That's fantasy."

"So what *do* you expect to find here?"

Ross continued staring out into the darkness. "I'm not sure. Some sense of where I came from. Of who I am. A place that feels comfortable." He turned away from the railing and faced Gordy. Ross's face was almost invisible in the darkness. "I guess I'm looking for home."

The two men sat quietly for a long time. The palm fronds scratched noisily. A cool breeze from the ocean brought the smell of salt water.

Finally Gordy spoke. "I hope you find it."

7

The next morning Ross woke up. He looked at his watch. Eight o'clock. He rolled over to see if Gordy was still asleep. The sheets were twisted. The bed was empty. Ross got up. Gordy wasn't in the living room and kitchen. Ross pushed the door open. Gordy was sitting at the table on the balcony. He had a cup of coffee in his hands. He looked up.

"Morning, partner. Want a cup of instant coffee? And a roll? They left rolls on our table at 6:30. The coffee was in the cupboard."

"How do you know they left the rolls at 6:30?" Gordy looked haggard. A day's growth of beard stained his chin. His hair was standing up in spikes. "By the way, you look terrible."

"Thanks for pointing that out. I know the guy left the rolls at 6:30 'cause I was sitting here."

"Couldn't sleep, eh?"

"No. And if you keep sleeping when I can't, I'm going to get real resentful."

"Sorry. You'll adjust. Jet lag, you know. You'll be fine in a few days. And remember: No one ever died of insomnia."

"That's reassuring. Actually it was kind of nice this morning. Look. You can see the ocean from here. I watched guys jogging early this morning. The mist rose off the ocean. It's sunny."

"It's always sunny at this time of year. It only rains from June to October."

"Great. Have a roll and let's head for the beach."

A high wall separated the grounds of the hotel from the beach. Next to a gate in the wall was a guard shack. A man in a red shirt printed with white elephants sat in the shack. A club like a small baseball bat hung behind him. He nodded to the two men as they passed through the gate.

The beach stretched north for several kilometres. To the south they could see several more hotels. A river flowed to the ocean a half kilometre away.

A man with a bag over his shoulder approached Gordy.

"Good morning, my friend." He extended his hand. Gordy shook it uncertainly. "Would you like to buy a few postcards?"

"Well," Gordy said uncertainly. "We just got here. I don't think so."

"But I have the best selection. And a very good price."

"I don't think so."

As he was talking another man walked up. He was carrying several carved masks. He had a gym bag over his shoulder. He held out his hand to Gordy.

"Hello, my friend. Would you like to see my carvings? I'll give you a very good price. A Gambia price."

Gordy looked around for Ross. He was standing several feet away grinning. A jogger passed by him. "Salammalekum," he said to Ross. Ross looked confused for a minute. He nodded uncertainly.

A large woman in a long blue and white printed dress walked quickly up the beach toward Gordy. A piece of cloth the same pattern as her dress was wrapped around her head. On top she carried a large basket of fruit. She pushed the carving and post-card sellers away.

"Hello my friend." She held out her hand. Gordy noticed three short scars in the black skin of each cheek. Her complexion was perfect. It was as if a light was glowing inside her face.

"I am Maria. Would you like some fruit? I have nice bananas. Groundnuts." She put her basket down. She picked up a pineapple and pressed it into Gordy's hand. "Just 20 dalassis."

Gordy held the pineapple awkwardly. "But I don't have any money," he pleaded. He thrust it back at her. "Here. I'll buy something later." He looked at Ross. "Jeez, Ross. Let's get out of here. I'm heading for the water."

He sprinted for the waves breaking gently several feet away. He ran into the water. It was warm. He walked through the shallow surf until it was up to his waist. Then he swam out farther. He bobbed gently in the green swells. He saw Ross swimming out toward him.

Suddenly he heard a voice near him. "Hello, my friend." An African was swimming out toward him.

"My God," Gordy shouted to Ross. "They've even got ocean-going hawkers."

Ross swam up beside him laughing. "They leave me alone. I guess they figure I'm a local. Let's swim for a while. Then let's head back in and walk the beach."

Walking the beach was not that easy. Hawkers selling everything from velvet paintings to coconut baskets swarmed around them. Especially Gordy. Other tourists lay on mats and watched in amusement.

Two kilometres north of their hotel the beach ended. A spit of red rock stuck out into the waves. Above them on a bank they saw a round white building. The roof was thatched with coconut fronds. A sign outside said "Buba's Beach Club."

"Think they got food there?" Ross asked.

"I'd settle for a cold beer. You got any money? Uh oh. Here comes a guy with a bunch of T-shirts. He's headed right for us. Let's get up to that club."

Ross and Gordy walked up the stones to the restaurant. The walls came up about three feet. Poles held up the roof. Rough wood tables crowded the stone floor. They went inside. The shade was mercifully cool after the blazing sun of the beach.

"Look, they *do* have beer. You got any money?" Gordy repeated.

Ross pulled out a few crumpled bills. "Yeah, but just enough for me, partner."

"Come on, man," Gordy whined. "Don't joke about this."

Ross laughed. "Yeah, I've got plenty."

A woman came up with a menu.

"I'll look at that later," Gordy said. "What kind of beer do you have?"

"We only have our local beer. Julbrew."

"Is it cold?"

"Yes."

"Bring us two. Fast."

Julbrew turned out to be light and refreshing. Gordy was pouring his second when he looked up at Ross.

"Did you notice anything when we were walking up the beach?"

"You mean that everyone is black?" Ross joked.

"No, no. I mean the white women. The tourists."

"What about them?"

"What about them? Most of them didn't have any tops on!"

"Really? I hadn't noticed."

"Yeah right. I'll bet."

"Did *you* notice how all the African women did have tops on? Funny, isn't it?

"What's that?"

"Well, when the Europeans first came to Africa, they called the Africans savages because the women went topless. Now the African women are all covered and the Europeans are half-naked."

Gordy snorted. "Strange world, eh?"

The waitress came back. "Would you like some food?"

The menu had several fish dishes. There was also roast chicken. It also listed "African Food." Ross asked about it.

"Oh, that changes every day. Today it's chicken domodah. That's with peanut butter."

"That sounds great. I'll have that."

The young woman shook her head. "Sorry. That won't be ready until one or two this afternoon."

"Oh well, just bring me the grilled fish."

Gordy nodded. "Me too."

Ross looked out through the open walls to the ocean. "You like this?"

"Except for all those guys on the beach selling stuff, it's great."

"Want to go to Banjul tomorrow?"

"Banjul? That's the capital? The biggest city?"

"Yeah. It's not far. There's a museum there I'd like to check out. And we can just poke around the town."

"Sure. OK. Tomorrow it's Banjul. But first we have to fight our way back to the Bungalow Beach."

8

Walking out of the hotel the next morning was like walking onto the beach. Men and women selling fruit, carvings, cigarettes and T-shirts crowded around tourists. A line of small stalls ran along a courtyard between the Bungalow Beach and the next hotel. They were hung with rolls of cloth, batik dresses and shirts. Women dressed in bright dresses beckoned. "Hello, my friend. Come and see my shop. Gambian prices." Other stalls were filled with carvings and masks. Drums with goat skin heads were stacked to the ceiling. Models of koras, a stringed instrument with a gourd body, hung from the cloth dividers. A silversmith worked over a charcoal fire.

Gordy made the mistake of stopping in front of a stall and looking. Immediately a large woman came out and extended her hand. "Come visit my shop." She pulled him into her stall. "Many nice things. Best prices." Gordy looked helplessly at Ross and disappeared.

Ross watched the activity in the courtyard. A few white tourists poked around the stalls. Shopkeepers called to them. Offering the best deals in The Gambia. But Gordy was right. Basically everyone *was* black.

A man in a loose short-sleeved shirt walked by. He was middle-aged. A big smile split his face. His light blue shirt was embroidered in gold around the neck. He wore a tan baseball hat. "J am ngam," he said.

Ross looked at him blankly.

"I sama?"

The man looked at Ross more closely. He started at his shoes and studied his jeans. He stared at the Bob Marley T-shirt Ross wore. "You're not Gambian," he said at last.

"No, no, I'm not," Ross said. "I'm from Canada."

The man's eyes opened wide. "Canada! Good country. Very helpful to The Gambia. Very cold."

"Yeah, in the winter. What did you say to me a few minutes ago?"

"I said hello in Wolof. When you didn't reply I tried Mandinka. You look Mandinka."

"Really? Can you tell what tribe different people are from."

"Of course." The man nodded with his head around the courtyard. "That man is Jola. Those two women over there are Wolof. The boys kicking the soccer ball are Mandinka. The woman selling fruit is Serahuli."

Ross was amazed. "How can you tell? I mean how do you know she is Serahuli?"

"Because she *looks* Serahuli."

"I see."

"Allow me to introduce myself," the man said formally. He pulled a worn card out of his shirt pocket. It read: "Sarjo Sanyang. Excellent Driver. Look for the white Lada. Always at your service."

Sarjo smiled a broad smile. "If you need me, ask the taxi captain for me." He began to walk off.

Ross hesitated. "Sarjo," he called after him. "Can you take us into Banjul?"

"Of course. Us?"

"My buddy is in the market."

Just then Gordy burst out of the stall. He had a shirt printed with crocodiles on over his T-shirt. He ran toward Ross. The woman shopkeeper hurried after him.

"What about your girlfriend? I have many nice dresses!"

"Get me out of here," Gordy hissed. "Before she sells me everything in the store."

"Nice shirt. The crocodiles are very becoming," Ross commented.

"Man, I had to buy something. She wouldn't let me out of there."

"Did you bargain?" Ross asked.

"Bargain?"

"Yeah. The seller starts high. Two or three times what she really wants. You have to haggle to get the price down."

"Yeah? I did think this seemed pretty expensive."

Ross laughed. "No wonder she wants you so bad. Here she comes."

"This way, gentlemen," Sarjo said.

"Who's he?" Ross asked, hurrying after him.

"Our taxi driver."

The woman stopped. Her hands were on her wide hips. "Come back," she called. "I'll be here tomorrow!"

Sarjo led them to an ancient white Lada. He opened the back door. The upholstery inside was covered with zebra-striped cloth. Ross and Gordy slipped in. Sarjo shut the door. Then he went around to the front and got in.

"Sarjo, how do I open the door?" Ross asked. "There aren't any door handles."

"No problem," Sarjo replied. "I'll open them for you."

Sarjo put the key into the ignition. He cranked the engine. It sputtered into life. The transmission whined as they pulled out into the road. The broken door to the glove box hung open. It shuddered as the car jerked forward. The black vinyl of the dashboard was cracked.

"How much to Banjul?" Ross asked.

"The regular rate is 75 dalassis. One way."

"One way! Man, that's almost 10 bucks!"

"But I'll make you a deal," Sarjo went on. "Give me 150 dalassis and I'll drive for you all day."

"You'll take us around?"

"Anywhere you want to go."

Ross looked at Gordy. Gordy nodded. "OK. Deal," Ross said.

The trip to Banjul was a rush of images for Ross and Gordy. The road passed by open shops where men were repairing tires. Stalls selling fruit were scattered along the highway. Other shops had squat toilets and sinks for sale. There were video stores. And a large white ice cream shop. Shops selling rice and canned goods dotted the road. Old Peugeots, Renaults and Mercedes Benzes whizzed by. The road was lined with palm trees and flowering shrubs. They were splashed with bright red and lavender.

But it was the people that most fascinated the men. Women, some with long dresses, others with wrap-around skirts and smocks, carried huge bundles on their heads. Others had babies strapped to their backs with a length of cloth. Some chewed on sticks. Some of the women's hair was braided in long plaits. Others had their hair tucked under a bright cloth wrapped around their heads.

The men were generally less colourful. Many wore dark pants and T-shirts. But some wore long-sleeved, ankle-length robes that looked like long night shirts. They were in almost every colour. Except green.

"Those robes the men wear," Ross began.

"In Mandinka we call them fataras."

"Why aren't there any green ones?"

"Green is the holy colour of Islam. Almost all Gambians are Muslim."

"Sarjo," Ross said. "You seem to know a lot of Mandinka."

"I know Mandinka, Wolof, Jola. A little Fula and Serer."

"Wow," Gordy commented. "I have enough trouble with English."

"But of course, I am Mandinka," Sarjo went on.

"You're Mandinka?" Ross asked. There was excitement in his voice.

"Yes. Forty percent of Gambians are Mandinka."

"That's why I'm here!" Ross began. Ross rattled off the story about General Maurepas. About discovering that his ancient ancestor was Mandinka. About his own quest to find his Mandinka roots.

Sarjo drove silently. "Many American blacks come here looking for their past," he said at last. "But they often find something else."

"What do you mean?"

"There is an old Gambian saying," Sarjo said. "It goes, 'However long the stump of a tree has been in the river, it will never become a crocodile.' "

"What does that mean?" asked Gordy.

Sarjo shrugged.

They had passed over a bridge and were entering the city of Banjul. Two-storey buildings rose around them. Most had metal roofs. Traffic became thicker. People crowded broken sidewalks. They went around a large field. "McCarthy Square," Sarjo informed them. "Cricket field."

Sarjo pulled onto a street. A woman walked by them with an enamelled bowl on her head. A large fish hung out on each side. A long building extended along the entire block. A balcony ran along the second storey. Along the sidewalk underneath the balcony dozens of little shops sold tapes, magazines and shampoo.

"Come on," said Sarjo. "We're going to Albert Market."

He led them along the dusty sidewalk to an arched entrance. Inside there was a maze of hundreds of stalls and shops. People pushed around them. They moved slowly toward the centre of the market. There a tree grew in the centre of a huge open circle. Tables were piled high with small bright red tomatoes, peppers and onions. Women shopped, putting their purchases in plastic tubs balanced on their heads or in woven bags.

Gordy crowded closer to Ross.

"What's wrong with you?" asked Ross.

"Man, I'm the only white guy here."

"Yeah? So?"

"People are staring at me."

"Ah, it's just your imagination."

They threaded their way through the cramped aisles between tables. Stalls selling fish laid out on tables appeared. Silver scales coated the planks. Large knives were stuck into the boards. Sarjo led them into a covered area. It was the butcher shop. Skinned goats hung from the ceiling. Chops of beef and goat filled the tables. Plucked chickens with their heads still on hung from their necks. Flies were everywhere.

"Man," Gordy said. "I couldn't eat that. Look at all the flies. Shouldn't they refrigerate this stuff?"

"I imagine you do eat it. Where do you think the restaurants get their meat?"

Outside the meat market they plunged into another maze of stalls. Beautiful dyed cloth was stacked high on 50 tables. Women unfolded eight foot lengths of batiked and tie-dyed cloth in hundreds of shades and designs.

"How much would those go for?" Ross asked Sarjo.

"If you bargain, 65, 70 dalassis."

"Oh, no," groaned Gordy. "I paid four times that for my shirt!"

Sarjo led them by men pressing white shirts with irons. For heat they filled the old irons with burning charcoal. They left through a long row of wood carving and leather shops. The owners saw Gordy and began to call to him.

One man brought out a handful of necklaces. They were shells sewn onto leather. They hung from a leather strand. Gordy stopped and looked at them. "How much?"

"Good price. Only 20 dalassis each."

Gordy turned away. "Nah. I'm not really interested."

The shopkeeper called to him in English: "Give me a price!" Gordy kept walking. Then the man started shouting angrily.

Gordy walked up quickly to Sarjo. "What's he yelling?"

"He's cursing you in Wolof. He says, 'White men don't bargain fairly.' "

"But I wasn't interested."

Sarjo shrugged. "You asked him the price. That meant you were ready to bargain. Then you walked off without giving your price."

"Bad form, eh?"

The men emerged back onto the road they had entered the market from. They walked up Russell Street, looking at all the little shops. Paint had worn from the plaster. Cracks in the uneven sidewalk were filled with red dust. Women vendors squatted on street corners and sold plastic bags of white cashews. They stopped at a little shop selling food. Sarjo recommended a spicy meat sandwich in flat bread. They ate as they walked.

They neared a three-storey modern building. It was flat on top. Colourful designs were worked into the walls in tile. A sign over the entrance read: The Gambia National Museum.

"The museum!" Ross said. "I need to go there. You guys mind?"

"What are you looking for?" asked Gordy.

"An island. I'll let you know if I find it."

9

"Gordy!" Ross was calling in a loud whisper. "I've got it!"

They had been in the National Museum for about an hour. Gordy had found the displays interesting. There were mortars for crushing millet. Sections on metal smithing contained delicate silver jewellery. There were also ancient swords. Gordy learned that spinning and weaving were jobs only men did.

There were 200-year-old staffs intricately carved with male and female figures. And little dolls carried by childless women to make them fertile. There were ancient board games called bau. The entire second floor was devoted to warfare. There were hundreds of masks, bows, and spears. A whole section was devoted to the Kaabu Empire. It was a Mandinka kingdom that lasted for 250 years. Ross had shown some interest in this. But he seemed impatient. He was looking for something else.

Finally they were on the third floor. This covered more recent events. Ross had disappeared into a room devoted to trade. He called Gordy again.

Gordy hurried into the room and looked over Ross's shoulder.

He was pointing at a map of Gambia and Senegal. The legend told them the map traced the export of slaves from the region. The arrows continued to North and South America. They showed where the people were sent: the United States, Haiti, other Caribbean islands, Brazil.

Ross had his finger against the plastic covering the map. "See!" he said excitedly.

Gordy looked more closely. Ross was pointing to a tiny island off the coast of Senegal. A wide black arrow indicated that hundreds of thousands of slaves has been shipped from there.

Gordy nodded his head. "Yeah. I see it. So what?"

"You remember Maurepas' story? Remember I said that he wrote he had been held on an island. It was Gore or Gory—I couldn't make it out, remember?"

"Yeah. I do."

"Well, here it is!" Ross said triumphantly. "It's Goree Island. That's where he was held. That's where he was shipped from!"

Ross raised his eyebrows. "Neat. Good detective work. You ready to leave now?"

Ross was agitated. "Yeah. I guess so. Let's go down and meet Sarjo."

Sarjo had decided to stay outside and visit friends. When they came outside he was across the street leaning against another taxi. When he saw Gordy and Ross he waved to the men he had been talking to. He walked across the street.

"Did you find anything interesting?" he asked.

"Yeah," Ross replied. "Goree Island."

"Ah. Centre of the French slave trade. I've been there."

"You've been there? What's it like?"

"Oh, yes. It's right near Dakar. You can take a ferry there. It's very pleasant. Many of the slave quarters have been made into restaurants. Homes. But some have been preserved as they were a hundred years ago. It's impressive."

They were almost back to the Lada. "Man," Ross mused. "I'd sure like to get there."

Sarjo unlocked the doors and let Ross and Gordy into the back seat. He got into the front and started the motor.

"I can take you there."

"Take us there?" Ross said. "By taxi? It must be more than 200 kilometres. It would cost us a fortune."

Sarjo shrugged. "I have relatives in Dakar. I need to see them anyway. I will charge you 150 dalassis a day. You pay for the gas."

Ross turned to Gordy. Gordy was peering out the window. "What do you think, Gordy."

Gordy gave a lopsided grin. "Look, I used to think Calgary was far away. Strange. Big. Now I'm in the middle of West Africa. It's once in a lifetime. So why not? You want to go to this Gory Island, I'll go too."

Sarjo drove by an enormous building. Four columns held up high arches. Two tall towers spiralled upwards on each side. The whole structure gleamed white in the bright sun.

"This is the new mosque," Sarjo told them. "That's a Muslim church. It is the largest building in Banjul."

"Wow," said Gordy. "It's beautiful."

Sarjo turned down a narrow, sandy road. "Do you gentlemen mind if I stop by my home before we go back to the hotel? I bought a bag of rice in the market. I would like to drop it off for my wife before dinner."

Gordy shook his head. "That's fine," Ross said.

A ditch ran down one side of the road. It was filled with grey water. The stench of sewage thrust through the open windows of the Lada.

"Yuck!" Gordy said, wrinkling his nose. "What's that?"

Sarjo looked out his side window. "That's our sewage system. In this part of town it's just open ditches. When it was built many years ago, the tide was supposed to flush it out. That never worked." Sarjo shrugged. "I don't even notice the smell anymore. But it's not healthy."

The Lada drove along the sandy road. Small shops dotted the roadside. Barefoot children in shorts and T-shirts ran along side of the car. "Toubob!" They called, pointing. "Toubob!"

"I think they're yelling at me," Gordy said uneasily.

"Indeed they are," Sarjo replied from the front. "Toubob means 'white man.' "

"Toubob!" the children chanted.

Gordy shrank back into the seat.

"Don't take it personally," Sarjo went on. "They don't mean anything. Not many white men come down into this part of town. You're just a curiosity to them."

"That makes me feel a lot better," Gordy said.

Sarjo pulled up beside the end of a long building. A 12-foot dirt walkway ran between two rows of red doors. The cement blocks of the building could be seen where the plaster had chipped off. There were eight or nine doors on each side. Women and children crowded the narrow courtyard. Clothes hung from ropes strung between the two rows.

Sarjo turned around and looked at Ross and Gordy. "This is my compound. This is where I live with my second wife," he said.

"Second wife?" Gordy asked. "You mean you've got more than one?"

"Oh, yes. But I only have two. Some Gambian men have three. The Koran—that's the Muslim holy book—allows a man to have four. My other wife lives in my village with the three older children. Although Aime—that's my oldest daughter—is here now." He opened the front door of the car. "Would you like to come in?"

"Sure," Ross said. "That would be nice."

Sarjo opened the back door of the Lada so Ross and Gordy could get out. Then he went to the trunk of the Lada and untwisted a piece of wire. The wire held the trunk lid down. He pulled the trunk open. He placed a stick under it to keep the lid up. A huge cloth sack of rice lay on the trunk floor.

"Boy!" Gordy exclaimed. "You're not kidding you bought some rice."

"Forty kilogram bag," Sarjo said. "It's not good rice. The grains are broken. But it is only 150 dalassis a bag."

Ross did some quick calculating. "At eight dalassis to the dollar, that's a little less than 20 cents a pound. That's still not cheap."

"Would one of you help me carry this in?" Sarjo asked.

Ross grabbed one end. Sarjo took the other. The bag was heavy. Ross's thick biceps stretched the sleeves of his T-shirt. He and Sarjo shuffled down the courtyard to a door halfway down the compound. Children stared curiously at them from open doors. A woman came out of the door where Sarjo had stopped. Sarjo put the bag down.

"Gentlemen, this is my wife, Jatu."

Jatu wore a brightly printed blue and gold skirt that went to her ankles. Above she wore a white tank top. She had a cloth wrapped around her head. It was the same pattern as her skirt. She was tall and slim. She smiled shyly and extended her hand. Ross took it. It remained limp. Then she extended her hand to Gordy. She didn't say a word.

Ross and Sarjo picked up the rice and carried it through the door.

The room inside was cool. Wooden shutters closed the only window. A metal double bed took up most of the cement floor. A simple dresser sat against the wall on their left. There was a door to another room next to the bed. The whole room could not have been more than 10 feet by eight feet. It was spotless. Nothing was out of place.

"Sit down," Sarjo said.

Gordy looked around uncertainly. A cluster of children crowded the door. They peered at him silently. He sat down on the bed.

"Babu, Ebrima. Come here," Sarjo said to the children at the door. Two boys stepped forward into the dark of the room. They were about 10 and 12. One wore pink gym shorts and a white collarless shirt with long sleeves. He had clear plastic sandals on his feet. The younger boy had a faded red T-shirt and long white pants on. He was barefoot. "Meet Mr. Gordy and Mr. Ross."

The two boys smiled shyly and extended their hands. Gordy and Ross shook them lightly.

"So, do you have several rooms?" Gordy asked.

"Just two. The children sleep in this room." Sarjo gestured through the open doorway. He shrugged. "We cook on a grate outside. There is a faucet for everyone in the compound. The rent isn't bad. Three hundred dalassis a month."

"Still," Ross pointed out. "That's almost $40."

"Yes. I'm lucky. I have the cab. In a good week I can make my rent." He shook his head. "Many people in The Gambia are not so lucky."

Just then a young woman stepped out of the shadows of the door to the back room. She stood quietly in the doorway.

Sarjo looked up. "Oh. And please let me introduce you to my oldest daughter, Aime. She is my daughter by my first wife. She has come from my village to live with us. She is very smart," he said proudly. "She is a modern woman. She is taking a secretarial course at The Gambia Technical Training Institute. Aime, this is Mr. Ross and Mr. Gordy. They are from Canada."

Aime stepped forward. Her skin glowed deep mahogany. Her eyebrows arched over big, dark eyes. Her hair was pulled back beneath a red batik cloth. Long silver earrings hung from delicate ears. She smiled. Her brilliant white teeth contrasted with her full dark lips. Gordy stood up from the bed. He shook her soft hand. Then Aime turned to Ross. Ross still stood in the middle of the room by the bag of rice. He stared at Aime. He seemed frozen. Aime moved gracefully to Ross. Her long batik dress was pulled tightly at her slim waist. A silver chain hung from her long neck.

"Ross, I believe?" she said, holding out her hand. "I'm surprised to meet a black man from Canada."

"Ross," Ross stammered. "Yes." He finally took her hand. "Actually, my parents were from Haiti. Glad to meet you."

Aime gave Ross her brilliant smile. "You'll have to excuse me," she said. "I'm meeting some friends. School's out. We're planning a party for next week." She smiled again at Ross and Gordy. "Very nice to meet you. How long are you here?"

Ross seemed unable to speak. "Another couple of weeks," Gordy said.

"Well, maybe we'll see each other again." She stepped around Ross and through the door. Ross turned his head and watched her.

"I certainly hope so," he said under his breath.

On the trip back to the Bungalow Beach Ross didn't say much. Sarjo tried to make plans for the trip to Senegal.

"Would you gentlemen like to leave tomorrow?"

Gordy looked at Ross. Ross stared out the window.

"How about the day after tomorrow?" Gordy asked. "That would give us a chance to get organized. And for me to get over my jet lag."

Sarjo nodded. "That would even be better." He hesitated. "I would like to make a request," he said. "If this is not fine with you I will understand. As I said, I have family in Dakar. It's actually my first wife's sister. Aime's aunt. Aime hasn't seen her for several years. She is out of school now. Would you mind if Aime came to Dakar with us?"

Ross seemed to emerge from a fog. He leaned eagerly over the seat. "Mind?" he blurted. "That would be great!" Gordy looked at him curiously. Sarjo stared at him in the rear view mirror.

Ross sat back. "I mean, that would be great for Aime. I mean to see her aunt. And all..." His voice drifted off. But he was grinning widely.

10

"Man, did you see her?" Ross asked. "She was the most beautiful woman I've ever seen. I mean it."

Ross and Gordy were sitting at Buba's Beach Club. They each had two empty Julbrew bottles in front of them.

"Who?" Gordy teased.

"Who? Who do you think? Aime!"

Gordy smiled. "She *was* pretty."

"Pretty? She was stunning. Have you ever seen skin like that? It almost glowed."

The waitress came up to their table.

"Uh, what's the African food today?" Ross asked.

"Chicken yassa. Chicken with lemon and onions."

Ross closed his menu. "I'll have that."

"Sorry. It is all gone."

Ross looked exasperated. "Last time it wasn't ready when we were here. Today it's all gone?"

The waitress shrugged. "I'll have the grilled fish," Ross sighed.

Gordy nodded. "And two more Julbrews."

It was early in the morning. Gordy and Ross waited on the porch outside their hotel lobby. They sat in heavy wood chairs covered in batik cloth. Sarjo had explained that they had to make the 9:00 a.m. ferry across the Gambia River from Banjul.

At exactly 7:30, the old white Lada swung through the gate to the Bungalow Beach. A plume of dust rose behind. Sarjo pulled up in front of the porch and waved. Aime sat in the front seat of the car with her father. Her shoulder-length hair was woven into dozens of tiny braids. It gleamed jet black. It was pulled back from her forehead. Her high cheekbones framed her broad smile. Ross's heart skipped a beat when he saw her. God, he thought. She's more beautiful than I remembered.

Sarjo unwired the trunk and held up the lid. Ross and Gordy threw in their bags. Then they got into the back seat. Aime turned toward them and rested her chin on the back of her seat.

"I sama," she said. "I be nyadi?" She looked right at Ross.

"I Sama. Nyadi. A baraka," he said.

Aime laughed in delight. "That's very good. We'll have you speaking in Mandinka in no time."

"What did you say?" Gordy asked Ross.

Ross beamed. He kept his eyes on Aime, who gazed back at him. "She said hello. Asked me how I was. I said fine. Then I thanked her."

"You taking Mandinka in night school?" Gordy asked.

Aime had turned around. Ross finally looked at Gordy. "Nah. Sarjo just wrote down a few words for me. I've been practicing."

Sarjo drove through Banjul into an area they hadn't been to

before. They drove around the waterfront. Old sunken ships jabbed out of the shallow harbour. Long, brightly painted fishing canoes were pulled up in sandy coves. A few large freighters docked at the end of several jetties. Finally they turned into the ferry terminal. A long line of cars and trucks was in front of them. Sarjo pulled into line and turned off the motor. Hundreds of people sat on bundles. Hawkers with everything from key chains to plastic sandals worked their way through the crowd. It was like a circus.

The hawkers converged on the car as soon as Sarjo turned off the ignition. Gordy shrank back into the seat. Young boys pressed cards with jackknives attached up against the glass. Women stuck fruit at them through Sarjo's open window.

"You know, Sarjo," Gordy said. "I just can't get used to people selling stuff all the time. They're always hustling. At least here they take no for an answer. On the beach they're so aggressive."

Sarjo shrugged in the front seat. "We are poor people," he said. "Many of these people have come from the villages. They think they will have a better life in the city. But it is hard. There are few jobs. They have no one to help them as they have in the villages. They struggle. They get a few dalassis together and buy something to sell. What else can they do?" He paused. "But you have made the problem on the beach."

Gordy looked surprised. "Me?"

"Tourists. Who has money in The Gambia? The tourists. So desperate Gambians flock there. They can't get jobs in the hotels. Or the restaurants. Only a few thousand are actually employed. So they try selling. Anything. And it's like a lottery. Do you have lotteries in your country?"

Gordy nodded.

"They all hope to hit the jackpot. Some European who will take pity on them and pay for their children's education. Who will take them back to England. Who will pay three or four times what they bought a shirt for. That is why there are so many on the beach. They are there like flies on cow dung." He shrugged again. "Like me."

There was no bitterness in Sarjo's voice. He was matter of fact. That's the way it was.

"There's an old saying in The Gambia," Sarjo continued. "Corn is different from a white man."

Gordy looked puzzled. "What does that mean?

Sarjo gave a little smile. He looked at Gordy in the rear view mirror. He shrugged. "Oh, look," he said. "Here comes the ferry."

An ancient car ferry clattered into the dock area. It had once been white. Now rust streaked the sides. But what amazed Gordy were the people on the decks. People with enormous bundles on their heads crowded among old cars. Big transport trucks were hidden by the mass of people. Women wrapped in bright cloth had babies strapped to their backs. There were crowds of men with red and blue toques on their heads. Goats strained at short ropes. The old ferry listed dangerously. It pulled into the dock. Workmen ran a metal ramp to the ferry. People streamed off. Then the trucks and cars sputtered into life. They nudged their way down the ramp barely avoiding the lines of people. Finally the ferry was empty. The waiting traffic moved slowly up the creaking ramp. Sarjo took them to the front of the ferry. He stopped a few feet away from a chain. The chain was all there was between them and the brown water of the harbour.

Once the vehicles were in place, foot passengers surged on board. Hundreds crammed every foot of available space. People pressed against the Lada's doors. They stood in front of the car. Gordy suddenly realized he had to go the bathroom. Bad.

"Uh, Sarjo," he said, squirming in the back seat. "Is there a bathroom on the ferry."

Sarjo snorted. "I don't know if you'd call it a bathroom. There is a place where people urinate."

Gordy didn't really like the sound of that. But he was desperate. "OK. So how do I get out of the car?" A dense wall of bodies held the doors shut.

"You would have to climb through a window."

Gordy stared at the mass of shoulders and bags filling the windows. He decided he'd try to wait.

The Gambia River was several kilometres wide here at its mouth. The low north bank was just a smudge through the windshield. The old ferry shuddered into life. It struggled away from the dock.

"Man, Sarjo. There sure are a lot of people on this thing."

"Oh, yes. It is the main river crossing. The next one is a hundred miles up river. At Farafenni. People who live on the North Bank must come this way. Also, this is the route to Senegal."

Gordy stared at the press of people surrounding the car. "But where are they all going?"

"Back to their villages. Maybe they were selling goods in Banjul. Visiting family. Some will take buses and trucks to Dakar."

"And how far is Dakar?"

"It is 200 kilometres from Banjul. One hundred and twenty miles or so."

Gordy was terrified the ferry would capsize under the weight of the crowd jammed on the decks. But Ross seemed unconcerned. He stared blankly out the windows. Other times, when Aime wasn't looking, he stared at her. He had a silly half-smile on his face.

The trip across the river took over half an hour. Gordy thought he would burst. When they finally arrived, the docking scene was played out again. Women passengers carrying enamelled basins or cloth bundles streamed down the ramp. Mixed in were men tugging goats. Sarjo started the Lada. He rolled carefully down the ramp through the crowd. He drove down a dusty road through a set of gates. He stopped.

"Here is a latrine," he said. He pointed at a small cement block building. "Hurry before the passengers get here. It will become very crowded."

Gordy did as he was told.

The road north to the Senegalese border wound along the river. Then it pushed north through dusty fields. Finally they came to a cluster of cement block buildings. The familiar red, blue and green flag of The Gambia flew on a pole in front. A wooden gate blocked the road. Sarjo stopped. Children selling small bags of cashews clustered around the car.

"We must get our passports checked," Sarjo said. He got out of the car. Aime and Ross followed him. Gordy rummaged through his Grizzlies gym bag. For a minute he panicked. He couldn't find his passport. But then he remembered. He had wrapped it in a sock. Somehow he had figured that would protect it.

Gordy pulled the blue passport out of the sock. He reached through the open window and opened the door from the outside. He stepped out into the blazing sun. Then he made his way to the low building. Sarjo was coming out as he went through the door.

Inside, a counter ran the length of the main room. Fans blew feebly against the heat. At least it wasn't so blindingly bright. Ross stood at the far end.

Gordy walked up to the counter. He put his passport down on the worn wood surface. A man in shorts and an open beige shirt opened Gordy's passport. He stared at it for a long time. Then he looked up at Gordy.

Gordy started to feel uneasy. "Is there anything, uh, wrong?"

The man continued staring at Gordy. He said something loudly in some language that was definitely not English. Another man sitting at a desk typing stood up. He was taller and wore the same open-necked beige shirt. He walked to the counter. The first man gave him Gordy's passport. He said something Gordy couldn't understand. The other man shook his head.

"Mr. Thomas," he said, closing the passport. "You must come with me. The taller man raised a section of the counter.

"But, but why?" The room had become absolutely quiet. Gordy felt panic rising inside himself.

"You've overstayed your visit. You were only allowed a 24-hour stay."

"Twenty-four *hours*!" Gordy wailed. "I told the guy at the airport 24 *days!*"

The official looked stern. A man with a rifle stepped out of the gloom by the entrance.

"You must come with me," the official repeated.

Gordy looked around desperately. Ross was still at the counter. He put his passport in the breast pocket of his shirt. "I better get Sarjo," Ross said. He turned and hurried through the entrance. Gordy was alone.

11

Gordy stepped out the front door of the Customs office. Sarjo was at his side. The bright sunlight mingled with the warmth of relief. Ross and Aime waited anxiously by the car.

Ross stepped forward when he saw Gordy. "They let you out. Man, I thought I was going to see you next in the Banjul penitentiary."

"I know what you mean. When that guy took me into that little office I was scared. I thought they were going shine lights in my eyes or something. You know, maybe they thought I was a spy."

"So what happened?"

"The guy sat me down on this wooden chair. Then he went behind his desk. He glared at me. He started by telling me they were very strict about permit violations. He pointed out that the penalties were harsh."

"Great."

"Yeah. That's what I thought. Then I heard Sarjo's voice. He was shouting out in the main room. Then the door opened. Sarjo walked in. He chatted with the guy. In Mandinka I guess. Pretty soon the customs guy started to smile. He shook hands with Sarjo. Then he stamped my passport and gave it back to me. He let us out the door. He even waved as we left!"

"Wow. What did you say to the guy, Sarjo?" Ross asked.

Sarjo gave his usual shrug. "He was Mandinka. I just explained that there was a misunderstanding. Besides, he is from the same district as my first wife. He knew her family. He knew her older sister very well."

Crossing into Senegal was comparatively easy. A flag with green, yellow and red vertical stripes flew outside of another building. There was a green star in the middle of the flag. The building looked a little newer. A little better kept up. The metal roof wasn't as rusty. The paint was fresher. Again children crowded around the car selling cashews. But they were all speaking French.

The road north to Dakar was blacktopped. But the land it wound through was dry and dusty. Traffic was light. Once they passed a passenger bus. Bundles were tied to the top. And to Gordy's astonishment a goat stood tethered on the roof. He faced forward and his ears blew back in the wind.

"Look at that!" Gordy pointed to the goat.

"Ramadan is coming soon. That is a Muslim holiday. Anyone who can afford to kills a goat. Someone is taking that one home."

"By how can he stand up there?" Gordy marvelled.

Sarjo shrugged. "Goats are very sure-footed."

They also passed old trucks piled impossibly high with hay. They groaned slowly along under their huge loads. The hay was twice as high as the cabs. They looked like cartoon trucks. Gordy couldn't see how they could stay upright. Then he saw one that had tipped over into a ditch.

Ross pointed at several high hills in front of them. They rose dramatically from the flat landscape. They looked like perfect cones.

"Look at those funny hills," he said. "They just seem to be stuck there."

Sarjo smiled. "Those are not hills. Those are groundnuts."

"Peanuts?" Ross and Gordy asked at the same time.

"That's right," Sarjo said. "Mountains of peanuts."

And they were. As the car passed, Gordy and Ross could see that the hills were actually huge mounds of peanuts. They rose several hundred feet.

Gordy sat back. Even with the window open the dry heat was wilting. Ross was leaning over the back of the front seat talking softly to Aime. Gordy's eyes began to droop in the heat. He dozed off.

When Gordy awoke the dry, flat scrub land had given way to buildings. Traffic was thicker. Colourful minibuses roared by. Gordy noticed that they had no glass in the windows. The name of the bus company and elaborate designs were painted on the outside. Passengers were crowded inside. Some stood on the bumpers and hung on by handles. The road widened. Buildings became higher. They encountered busy intersections. Sarjo wound his way through Dakar. Some streets were broad and tree-lined. Others were narrow. There were sprawling markets. Paper and dust filled the gutters.

Sarjo drove around a broad circle. High buildings ringed the round park. A fountain was in the middle. It wasn't working.

"This is the Place de l'Indépendence," Sarjo told them as they maneuvered through traffic. "It is the centre of the city. Your hotel is just over here." He swung wide and drove down a side street. Cars were parked on the broken sidewalks. Sarjo pulled up in front of the hotel. He got out and unwired the trunk. He took out Gordy's and Ross's bags. He put them beside the car.

Ross finally pulled himself away from Aime. He got out and walked back to the luggage.

"Look around Dakar," Sarjo told them. "But don't carry any valuables. Leave them in the hotel safe."

Gordy looked at him quizzically.

"Pickpockets," Sarjo went on. "Dakar is known for pickpockets. Especially around the Place de l'Indépendence. Especially at night." Sarjo shut the trunk lid and wired it shut. "Just be careful."

"Right," Gordy said.

"Aime and I will be staying with her aunt. No phone, of course. We'll see you here at 9:00 in the morning. Then we'll drive down to get the ferry to Goree Island. Good night."

Sarjo got back into the car. He drove off. Aime waved.

"Interesting city, eh?" Gordy asked.

Ross and Gordy were sitting at a cafe along the main street.

Glass surrounded them. Two bottles of local beer sat on the table in front of them. The traffic outside was thick.

"I think I'm in love," Ross said.

Gordy nodded. "You certainly display all the characteristics. Goofy grin. Staring off into space a lot. That sort of thing."

"Do you think I could stay here? You know, get married and settle down. In West Africa?"

Just then a man in a wheel chair rolled up to the window beside them. He held up his hands. He had no fingers. There were only blunt stumps where the thumb and fingers should be. He thumped on the glass.

A waiter came over and yelled at the man. He wheeled slowly away.

Gordy stared after him. "What was that?"

"Leprosy," Ross answered. "It's still common in Africa."

Another man came up to the glass. He held up a board full of watches. "Real Rolexes!" he yelled.

Gordy drank the last of his beer. "It's getting late," he said. "Let's head back to the hotel."

It was almost dark when they left the cafe. Gordy shook his head. "I can't get used to nightfall around here. One minute it's light, the next it's dark."

They walked down the boulevard. Worn trees grew through uneven cement. Hawkers called out from doorways.

It was almost completely dark by the time they reached the Place de l'Indépendence. Their hotel was on the other side.

Suddenly two men walked out from a side street. They held a few silver bracelets out.

"Bracelets," one man said. He walked alongside Gordy. "Good price." His hand seemed to brush against Gordy's rear pocket. The other man was just behind them.

"Not interested," Gordy said curtly.

The man suddenly reached for Gordy's runners. "Nice shoes. Want to sell them?"

Gordy stopped and bent over. He pushed the man's hands away. Instantly the man trailing them grabbed at Gordy's rear pants pocket. Gordy shoved the first man away. He went sprawling on the sidewalk. Then he turned toward the other man. He was already running back into the dark side street.

A whistle blew behind them. The man on the sidewalk jumped up and ran after his companion. An overweight man in a uniform puffed up. He was still blowing his whistle.

The whole incident had taken a few moments. Gordy stood staring after the two pickpockets. He was breathing heavily. Ross took a few steps after them and then stopped.

"Did they get anything?" the policeman asked. "Check your pockets. They are very clever."

Gordy felt his rear pocket. He smiled. "They got a folded map of Dakar."

"Is that all? Are you sure?"

Gordy felt his front pockets. "That's it. We left our wallets and stuff at the hotel."

"Good," the policeman said. "That is good." He shook his head. "I am sorry for this. Please forgive my countrymen."

He turned and ran down the street where the two men had disappeared.

Gordy could still feel the adrenaline racing through him. Ross grabbed him by the shoulder.

"You OK?"

Gordy nodded. "Yeah. Just a little shaken up."

"Come on. Let's cut across the Place to our hotel. We have to get up early in the morning anyway."

The two men walked quietly through the park. Paths had been worn in the grass. The fountain was filled with dust. Broken steps led down to the far side of the circle. They walked warily across the circle road and down the street toward their hotel. The twisted trunks of strange trees curled up into the night. Their glossy leaves were black. In front of their hotel a line of six or seven beggars eyed them. The beggars sat on small mats. Some chanted lowly, rocking back and forth.

Gordy hurried into the lobby. Ross was close behind.

12

Ross stood at the front of the small ferry. They had left the ferry terminal at Dakar harbour 20 minutes earlier. Ahead of him Goree Island was a smudge on the horizon. He stared across the water. What had this trip been like for his ancestor? Chained together with other desperate slaves. Leaving his people and land behind. Facing an uncertain future.

Slowly the island began to emerge from the sea. It was not large. Maybe one and a half kilometres long. A hill rose at the western end. Rows of low buildings appeared along the waterfront. They were plastered on the outside. They gleamed white and blood red in the bright sun. A broad walkway and stone sea wall ran around the edge of the island. Palm trees like green balls on sticks lined the walk.

Soon the ferry passed inside a stone levee. It made its way to a pier that extended out from shore. It pulled alongside. Men on the dock caught thick brown ropes thrown from the ferry. They tied them to rings. A plank was rolled over the side to the wharf. People began to crowd off the ferry. Ross watched.

It was a mixed crowd. Middle class Senegalese coming over for a picnic. White tourists. Local residents of the island with bundles of goods and sacks full of food. There was even a group of black American tourists. They talked noisily as they surged off the boat. One heavy man wore a Mickey Mouse T-shirt with "Disneyland" written on it. What were they thinking? Ross wondered. What were any of them thinking?

Even the island itself seemed to have forgotten its awful past. The passengers walked off the dock to a sandy cove. Children swam in the blue water. Clothes were hung on the brightly-painted fishing boats pulled up on the white sand. Around the cove French colonial buildings clustered about a square of flat stones. The old buildings were painted bright pastels. Wood shutters were closed against the heat. An ancient Catholic church occupied one end of the square. Its big wooden doors were open. The interior was dark and shadowy. Restaurants and pubs were strung around the square. Long tables were set up with gaily printed blue and red table cloths. White umbrellas shaded the tourists sipping beer from the bright sun. Was this the same Goree Island where hundreds of thousands of terrified slaves were sent to the New World?

"Come on," Sarjo said. "Let's walk around."

The walk Ross had seen from the ferry almost circled the island. It was broad, and at its edge a stone sea wall dropped directly down to the water. Narrow alleys wound between old buildings. People's wash was hung from lines between buildings. They could smell wood smoke from cooking fires.

The buildings were all two storeys. They fronted on the twisting alleys. They looked like very old warehouses.

"The slaves were kept in the bottom," Sarjo said softly. "The traders lived above."

"Who lives in them now?" Gordy wondered.

"Senegalese. Several hundred people live here year round."

"In the old slave quarters?" Ross asked.

Sarjo shrugged. "People have to live somewhere."

They walked up a path through older homes. Many of these had fallen into disrepair. The trail led up the hill Ross had seen on the ferry. At the top they could see Africa curving away to the south. The island spread out below them. From the height of the hill they could see how the warehouses were built close to the water around the protected edge of the island. "So they could move the slaves and other goods to the waiting ships," Sarjo explained.

The trail down led through bright hedges of deep red bougainvillea. Purple, yellow and white hibiscus grew in huge bushes in tiny back yards. The path turned into a cobblestoned alley. The walls of the homes and warehouses began to shade the narrow road. They wound down toward the heart of the island. Sarjo seemed to know where he was going. Gordy followed closely. He chatted with Aime. Ross trailed behind.

Sarjo stopped in front of an old warehouse. It looked like all the others. But outside the door there was a small booth.

"Here," Sarjo said. "This is the only slave quarters that has been kept as it was. It is a museum."

Gordy paid the small entrance fee. They walked in.

The building was little more than a gloomy set of large cells. The walls and floor were constructed of stone. The cells had tiny windows high in the walls. Signs explained that one cell had been for men. Another one had held women. And a small cell was for the children.

The cells were cold and bare. There was no latrine. No beds. Nothing. Slaves were held here for months.

They wandered through the dank stone corridors from room to room. Ross walked away from the group. A deep horror was seeping into him from the stones. He could almost feel the terror of the slaves. He didn't know how much longer he could stay.

He rounded a corner. On his left was a short, low passage. It ended in an open doorway. Only the sea was beyond. A single light above the door lit the gloomy passageway. Ross stared out on a narrow rectangle of water.

Something broke inside him. He could feel tears sting his eyes. Next to the passageway a simple paper sign had been stuck to the wall. It was in French. It read, "From this doorway, the slaves began a trip without return. Their eyes looked out on a sea of endless misery." Ross looked down the passage. So short and so long. He could hear screams, cries. He heard moaning and shrieks. The terror was suffocating.

Sobs rose in Ross's chest. He couldn't breathe. Tears streamed down his cheeks. He turned away down another corridor. It led to a bright courtyard. He leaned up against a stone wall and fought to catch his breath.

Aime emerged from the passage. She walked up to Ross. Hesitantly, she raised her hand to his face. She gently brushed the tears from his cheeks. They said nothing.

Gordy and Sarjo joined them. Gordy's usual smile was gone. His face was set and grim.

"Come," Sarjo said quietly. "Let's go out into the sun."

They left the building. Sarjo led them along the road back to the main village. The square was shining in the sun. Children laughed as they swam in the cove. Hawkers sold T-shirts and hats with pictures of Goree Island on them. Sarjo took them along the walkway a short distance. He stopped at an outdoor cafe. He motioned to the wood benches. They sat down. Umbrellas shaded them. The sea lapped gently against the stone wall below the walkway. A smiling waiter brought them menus. Sarjo ordered fish for them in French. Aime and her father spoke softly. Ross stared out over the ocean.

"I don't know how you can stand it, " Gordy said angrily. "How can you just sit there? Doesn't seeing those slave quarters make you furious?"

Sarjo shrugged. "What would you like us to do? That was a long time ago. We must live for the present. Not the past. Would getting angry help?"

Gordy shook his head. The waiter came back with their food.

"Four beers," Gordy said.

"Not for me," Sarjo said. "Muslims don't drink alcohol."

"Or me," Aime said. "Just fruit juice, please."

Gordy was still upset. "Well, bring four anyway," he snarled at the waiter. "I'll drink them."

Gordy looked at Ross. "And what about you?" he asked. "You haven't said a thing."

Ross looked at the three people at the table. His face was hard. His dark eyes seemed black.

"I don't know what to say," he said at last. "I'm all jumbled up inside. Fury. Sadness. Loneliness…" His voice trailed off. His right hand lay on the blue table cloth. Aime put her hand softly over his.

The meal was quiet. The seagulls squalled overhead. A breeze shook the palm fronds. The sea lapped at the sea wall.

A loud whistle sounded from the dock.

"That's the ferry," Sarjo said. "If we want to get back to Gambia tonight, we need to leave now."

Ross seemed to shake himself. "Let's go," he said. "I've seen enough."

They paid for their meals and hurried back to the boat.

When the ferry landed at Dakar, they made their way to Sarjo's Lada. Gordy and Sarjo walked ahead. Aime and Ross walked close together behind.

Gordy glanced behind them. "Uh, Sarjo. Mind if I ride up front with you on the trip back?"

Sarjo shrugged. He unlocked the front door for Gordy. Ross and Aime sat in the back.

Sarjo hurried through the congested city. Outside of Dakar he drove as quickly as he could. "The last ferry to Banjul leaves at 7:00," he explained. "If we miss it we sleep in the car."

Gordy looked at the dusty landscape. "Can you go any faster?"

The tire went flat just outside of a small city called Kaolack. The car swerved. Then they heard the tire slapping loudly. Sarjo pulled over.

"Where's your spare, Sarjo?" Gordy asked. "I'll help you change it."

Sarjo looked out of the windshield. He shrugged. "Spare's flat."

"The spare's flat? Sarjo, you can't drive out here with no spare!"

Sarjo shrugged again. He got out of the car and unwired the trunk. He propped it open with the board. Then he pulled his jack out. He jacked up the car and removed the wheel.

"I'll be back soon," he said. And he rolled the tire down the road toward the town.

Although it was late afternoon, the sun was still hot. The car became unbearable. Ross and Aime joined Gordy on the side of the road. Two boys walked by holding six live chickens by their feet. The upside down chickens peered curiously at Gordy. The boys stopped. "Poulet?" they asked.

"Non, merci," Ross said.

"Now they're trying to sell me live chickens?" Gordy asked.

"Maybe you looked hungry," Ross suggested.

It was over an hour before Sarjo appeared with the tire.

"Sorry," he said as he rolled it up to the car. "The nearest tire repair was several miles."

He bolted the tire onto the wheel. Then he lowered the jack and stored it in the trunk. They got in the stifling car. It smelled of melting vinyl and old oil. Sarjo began to drive.

"Sarjo," Gordy asked. "Are we going to make the ferry?"

"No."

"Great," muttered Gordy. "So what are we going to do?"

"There is another ferry, a hundred miles up river at Farafenny. It runs until 9:00. We may be able to make it. If we hurry."

"What about your spare?" Gordy asked. "Aren't you going to get it repaired?"

Sarjo shrugged. "No time."

Gordy nodded. "Great. We're heading into the interior of Africa. On a side road. It's getting dark. And we don't have a spare. Just great."

Now Sarjo drove furiously. Gordy didn't know the old Lada could go so fast. The speedometer was the only instrument that worked. It rarely dropped below 110.

They blasted through villages, scattering people and livestock. Soon it grew dark. The Lada's feeble lights barely illuminated 10 feet of road ahead of them. Sarjo saw donkey carts at the last minute and just swerved around them. He dodged the biggest potholes and slammed into others. Pedestrians jumped off the road in fright. Gordy peered anxiously through the windshield. Suddenly he screamed.

Sarjo slammed on the brakes. The car slid to a stop. Two feet in front of them a herd of 50 cattle filled the narrow road. A man in a white robe stared at them in terror. He used his staff to scatter the cows. Sarjo roared on.

At 8:45 they reached Farafenny. It was a row of low shops and houses made from mud bricks and concrete blocks. They stopped and bought their ferry tickets at a building on the side of the road. It was lit with candles.

"No power after 7:00," Sarjo explained. "Shut the generator down."

They drove further. A low shed with a porch was on the left of the road. "Customs," Sarjo said. "We've re-entered Gambia. Do you want to get your passport stamped?"

"Damned right," Gordy declared.

"Hurry," Sarjo urged.

Ross and Gordy entered the building. A lone man was slumped over a desk. A candle burned beside him.

"Is he sleeping?" Gordy asked.

"Or dead."

"That's all we'd need. I'm going to try to wake him up."

Gordy walked over to the man. He shook him gently by the shoulder. The man awoke slowly. He looked at them sleepily.

Gordy hurriedly explained their situation. The man took their passports without a word. He stamped them. Then he scribbled something. He handed them back. He lay his head back on his arms and was asleep again.

Gordy and Ross rushed back to the Lada and jumped in. Sarjo gunned the motor. They leapt down the road.

The road dropped down noticeably. Soon they could see lanterns in front of them. There was a short line of cars and trucks in front of them.

"Made it," Sarjo sighed.

"Which is more than you can say for about 40 goats you took out," Gordy joked.

The ferry began loading almost immediately. It was a single flat deck. As they drove on Gordy looked through his window. Dugout canoes were pulled up on the river bank. Men sat around a fire talking. A brown dog curled at the men's feet. It was a scene that could have been a thousand years old.

As the ferry rumbled into life, the captain shut off the lights. He steered by a single spotlight that shone a 10-foot circle on the water ahead. Except for that, the darkness was complete. Gordy got out of the car. The night was soft, velvety. He could almost touch it. A million brilliant points of light pricked the ink-black sky. Sarjo stood by his side. The thick night seemed to muffle sounds.

"How far to Banjul?" Gordy asked. He spoke in a low voice, almost whispering.

Sarjo shrugged. "Two hours."

Gordy nodded. He turned back to the car to tell Ross. Ross was against the far door asleep. Aime leaned against him. Her head was on his shoulder. Her eyes were closed. Gordy smiled. He turned back to the railing.

"It's a beautiful night," he said to no one in particular.

13

"You sure you don't want to go?" Ross asked again. It was two days after they had returned from Dakar. Ross and Gordy sat on the veranda in front of their room. On the plastic table, bright orange papaya halves lay on dishes. "She invited both of us."

Gordy sipped his instant coffee and looked out over the sea. "Nah. Really, man, I'm bushed. All I want to do is take it easy tonight."

Ross fingered an envelope. One of the hotel staff had brought it to the room that morning. It had been left by Sarjo at the front desk. It was an invitation from Aime. She asked them to join her and her friends that night at the school year-end party. It was being held at a club in Banjul.

"What'll you do?"

Gordy sat back and smiled. "Just what I want to do. Walk on the beach. Go down to the bar and drink a few Julbrews. Go to bed early and not have to listen to you snore." He smiled wider. "It'll be great."

Ross looked uncertain. "You're sure?"

"Absolutely. Anyway, I don't want to cramp your style."

Ross grinned. "OK. I'll let you know how it turns out."

When Gordy got up the next morning Ross was asleep in the bed next to him. Gordy hadn't even heard him come in. He tiptoed to the bathroom and shut the door quietly. He showered, dried off and shaved. He poked his head out the door. Ross was still snoring contentedly. Gordy got dressed quietly. He went to the kitchen and cut open a couple of mangoes.

They and Maria the fruit lady had become good friends. Every morning she waited by the hotel gate for them. She carried a woven basket full of fresh fruit. At first Gordy had bargained hard. Maria would wail about how much things cost at the market. How her husband had left her for a younger wife. How she had to bring up her two children by herself. But she always smiled. Now Gordy just picked out what he wanted and asked how much. And she stopped doubling what she really wanted to get. Just to stay in practice, sometimes he would open his eyes wide and say, "That much?" Maria would giggle and drop the price. At least the other fruit sellers left him alone.

Gordy took the mangoes and a cup of coffee onto the veranda. He read a book. In the background he heard the sea curl up on the sandy beach. The breeze from the ocean whispered through the palm fronds.

Ross lurched through the door. He fell into one of the white chairs across from Gordy. He laid his head on his arms. "Oh," he groaned. "God, what a night. Palm wine. Glasses of it."

Gordy looked up from his book. He glanced at his watch. "Another hour and you would have been up at the crack of noon." He studied Ross's face buried in his thick brown arms. "By the way, you look terrible."

"Thanks," Ross mumbled. "I appreciate your support."

"Now what's this about palm wine?"

Ross's face contorted in pain. "I don't want to talk about it."

"Fine. Fine. I'll just sit over here and mind my own business. You did say you would share the evening with me. But that's OK."

"Oh, shut up," Ross groaned. "I'll tell you all about it. But let's get some fresh air. Let's walk up to Buba's."

"Sure you're able to walk?" Gordy asked helpfully. "That means having to put one foot in front of the other, you know."

Ross opened one eye. "You're just being mean because you know I'm too hung over to strangle you."

Gordy stared up at the sky for a moment. "Possibly," he agreed.

"OK, don't tell me," Ross said to the waitress at Buba's. "The African food isn't ready."

"No, it's ready."

"OK, OK, then it's all gone."

"No. We still have some."

Ross looked up at the woman. "Really? Well, what is it?"

"Ladyfish cooked in palm wine."

Ross groaned and held his head. "Just bring me a Julbrew."

Ross had both elbows on the table. His fingers propped up his forehead. "So, as I was saying, they kept bringing this stuff for me to drink. It's a wine fermented from palm juice. They tap the palm trees. Kind of like maple sap. Then they ferment it."

"How's it taste?"

"Terrible. Like sour beer."

"So why'd you keep drinking it?"

Ross looked up miserably. "I don't know. Most of the girls sat together. And the guys sort of hung out. I was feeling out of place enough. I thought I should at least drink with them."

"So why'd you feel weird?"

"I don't know, man. When guys came up to me they'd rattle off something in one of the local languages. Aime said it was Wolof. And I'd stare blankly at them. I didn't know what the hell they were saying. They'd look kind of puzzled. One guy got mad. He yelled something at me! One of the other guys said something to him. He walked off. Still seemed pissed."

"Were some of the guys nice?"

"Oh, yeah. Friendly. But, you know, they talked about Gambia. Politics. The economy. Local jobs. What the hell do I know about that stuff?"

"What about Aime?"

For the first time Ross smiled. "You should see that woman dance."

"Nice, eh?"

"Nice? When they dance, they dance. And she was like a cat. Fluid. Sexy. Shaking her shoulders. Pumping her legs. Her face glowing with sweat." Ross looked up with bloodshot eyes. "Man."

"Yeah? And then what?"

"Things finally wound down. She took me for a walk on the beach. The moon was bright. Have you noticed the nights here? They're like black velvet. It just wrapped around us. Man..."

"So did you make love with her?"

"None of your goddamned business," he said. But his smile widened. His eyes drifted up. He stared over Gordy's shoulder. "When I held her, her skin felt like silk. Beautiful dark silk. And when I ran my hands down her back, her muscles were like steel." Ross sighed. "She's gorgeous."

"Whoa there, partner. Cool off!" Gordy poured them each a Julbrew.

Then Ross's eyes cleared. His smile faded. He looked directly at Gordy.

"I asked her to come to Canada with me," he said.

Gordy choked on his beer. "You what?" he spluttered. "What did she say?"

Ross breathed deeply in and out. "She asked me how many black people lived in the town I was from. How many times she would be able to come home."

"What did you say?"

"What could I say? And then she said that in Gambia her history and culture lived all around her. That in Canada she would be cut off from all of that. And from her family. In Canada, she said, she would be an oddity." He paused. "She said she would be like a fish on the beach. And then she said she had to stay and help her family. That they would not want her to leave."

Gordy sipped his beer. "How'd you respond to that?"

"I told her to screw her parents. She was an adult."

Gordy nodded. "That was smooth. Very, very smooth."

Ross shook his head. "I know. I was desperate, man. She was shocked. You could see it in her eyes."

"I'm not surprised. You know how important family is over here."

Ross held his chin in his hands. He looked miserable. "I apologized."

"Good. That was a good move."

He sighed again. "Then she asked me if I would stay here with her."

Gordy choked on his beer again. "Here? Stay here? What did you say?"

Ross shrugged. "Nothing. Yet. Then she asked if we would like to visit her village. To meet her mother. See her community."

Gordy pulled his hand through his hair. "Man, this is getting a little out of hand."

Ross laughed. "Nah, it's not like that. She and Sarjo were going up anyway. Sarjo hasn't seen his first wife or their kids since December. She asked me if we wanted to come. It would be a chance to see rural Gambia. The way people really live. It's just a visit. You up for it?"

Gordy grinned. "Wouldn't miss it for the world. When are we leaving?"

Ross looked at Gordy gratefully. "Day after tomorrow."

14

Sarjo picked them up in front of the Bungalow Beach early. Aime sat in the front. Her beautiful smile spread across her face when she saw Ross.

"It would be nice if you gave a present to our chief," Sarjo said as Ross and Gordy got into the Lada. "He is called the alkallo."

Ross was talking across the back seat to Aime. "Sure," Gordy nodded. "What do you suggest?"

"It is traditional to bring a sack of sugar."

Gordy punched Ross on the shoulder. Ross looked at him. His eyes were sparkling.

"Ross, a bag of sugar for the alkallo?"

"Fine by me."

"We'll get it here before we go," Sarjo said. "Cheaper."

Sarjo drove deep into the crowded streets of Serakunda. He stopped across from a small shop. A metal awning propped up by poles extended over a broken walkway. Bags were piled on each side of the open door.

"The shop owner is a Serahuli," Sarjo explained. "Good traders. But you have to watch them. I know him. He will be fair."

Sarjo got out. He opened Gordy's door from the outside. Gordy got out and walked across the road. Then Sarjo went to the back and unwired the trunk. He held it open with the stick. Sarjo led Gordy into the shop.

On their left more bags were piled up to the rafters. A short counter ran along the other side. An ancient cash register sat on the counter. A man in a long white gown and a white cap approached Sarjo. They began to bargain. Gordy wondered why there was all this fuss about a bag of sugar.

At last Sarjo nodded. He turned to Gordy. "I got a good deal. 160 dalassis."

"One hundred and sixty dalassis?" Gordy asked. "That's almost 20 bucks! I thought we were buying a bag, not the factory."

Sarjo shrugged. Gordy pulled the money out of his wallet reluctantly. He gave it to the man in the white gown. The man smiled. He had a gold front tooth.

Sarjo walked over to a stack of bags. "Give me some help?"

"This is it?" Gordy looked at the bag in surprise. "This must be nearly 50 pounds!"

Sarjo nodded. "Twenty kilograms."

"Sarjo, what the hell's the chief going to do with 45 pounds of sugar?"

Sarjo shrugged. Gordy took one end of the bag. They carried it across the street to the car. They slung it into the trunk.

The road to Sarjo's village started well. The blacktop was new.

The shoulders were red dirt. There was no centre line. But there were few holes. They drove through villages along the road. The homes were built of mud bricks or sticks. The roofs were palm thatch or metal. They were generally very small. Not more than 70 or 80 square feet. Sometimes the units would be attached. There was a line of doors. Sometimes they would be in a "U" around a small courtyard. Sarjo explained that this was a compound. A man and his wives and children would live there. Often his parents and even grandparents would live with them as well.

The homes in one village were round. The thatched roofs were like cones set on top. "Jola village," Sarjo commented. "Jola homes are always round."

Soon the road deteriorated. Potholes became more frequent. And they were larger. At some points there were more holes than road. Drivers drove along the dusty shoulders.

Several hours later Sarjo slowed at an intersection with a dirt road. He turned left. A small town of low buildings spread along both sides of the dusty road. Sarjo stopped.

"I must get some rice for my family," he said.

Ross was paying attention for a change. "We'll buy it. As a gift." He looked at Gordy. "It's the least we can do."

Ross and Sarjo disappeared into a building. Children with plates of cut mangoes and small bags of peanuts approached the car. They held the plates up to the car almost shyly. What a difference, Gordy thought, between these kids and the beach vendors.

Sarjo and Ross reappeared lugging the heavy bag of rice between them. They threw it into the trunk beside the sugar.

The road ran straight through dusty scrub land. Thin sandy soil supported a few stunted trees and bushes.

"You should see this in the rainy season," Sarjo said. "It is all green. Lush."

Gordy stared out the open window. The landscape was bleak and dry. He wasn't sure he believed Sarjo. He noticed 10-foot cones of red dirt rising out of the ground.

"Sarjo, what are those?"

"Termites. Those are termite nests."

"Termites. Yipes. Wouldn't want to have a wooden leg out there."

The road was crossed with deep washboard ruts. The old car clattered and creaked as Sarjo sped over the rough surface. The dirt road extended off for kilometres over the flat terrain. There were no houses.

"Uh, Sarjo," Gordy asked. "Did you get the spare fixed?"

The car skittered over a set of particularly deep ruts. Sarjo shrugged. "No time."

They sped down the dirt road for another hour. Fine red dust blew in a column behind them. It filled the car. Gordy considered raising the windows. But it was 40 degrees outside. He decided he preferred the dust.

They passed through occasional villages. Each was a cluster of small homes. In the middle of each community there was a water pump. Women in printed dresses filled pails and washed clothes nearby.

At last Sarjo slowed by a narrow dirt track. Gordy could see buildings along the road. This village was bigger than most of the others they had been through.

"Welcome to Manduar," Sarjo said. He turned off onto the track. Houses crowded along the road. Kids waved and ran alongside the car. Sarjo waved back. Gordy heard some of the children yelling, "Aime! Aime!"

Sarjo stopped in front of a low wall made of mud bricks. On each side a higher fence made of tall sticks enclosed the compound. Now 30 or 40 kids filled the courtyard. Most of them wore shorts. The older girls wore skirts. Some of the children had on old T-shirts. Many were ripped. Some had big holes. Gordy wondered why they wore them at all.

The kids crowded around the car. They grinned and waved. Sarjo got out and opened the back doors. Ross and Gordy stepped out into the withering heat. Aime got out of the front. Ross walked around to her. He put his arm around her shoulder. Aime looked at him in dismay. She shook his arm off her shoulders. "Not in public," she hissed. "Not here." She pulled away. Ross looked bewildered.

Sarjo led them through an opening in the wall into the courtyard. The kids parted but still stared. Especially at Gordy. Some pointed. "Toubob," he heard some of the children call quietly.

"Man, I'll never get used to it," Gordy muttered to Ross.

"What's that?"

"Getting stared at all the time. I feel like a curiosity. Something strange and exotic."

"Ah, you're just too sensitive. They're not staring. They're just curious. There aren't many white guys around here."

Gordy looked up at the crowd of black faces. "Thanks for pointing that out."

A low building about 30 or 40 feet long stretched across the small courtyard. There were four metal doors. Single metal-shuttered windows opened next to each door. The compound was made of mud bricks. It had been painted white a long time ago. A rusting metal roof slanted over the structure. A tall thin woman stood in front of one of the metal doors. She had on a long printed skirt. On top she wore a loose white sleeveless blouse. Her head was covered with a printed bandanna.

Sarjo walked up to her. She smiled at him. He turned to Ross and Gordy.

"This is my first wife, Juka," he said simply.

Gordy and Ross extended their hands. She took them hesitantly. Aime rushed up beside her father. The mother's eyes lit up. She smiled widely. Aime said something to her mother in Mandinka. Then they disappeared through the open door.

"This is my compound," Sarjo said. "My sons and daughter stay in each room. My wife and I share this one." He motioned to the door Aime and Juka had just entered.

He took them to another door. It was just a piece of roof metal nailed to a wood frame. "This is where you will stay. My oldest son, Lamin, is away. He is training to be a community health worker." Sarjo beamed proudly. "You will have his room."

Behind them children had carried their bags from the Lada.

They set them down behind Ross and Gordy. Gordy pulled a few dalassis from his pocket. He gave them to the children. Their eyes grew wide. They giggled and ran back to the other kids still crowded into the courtyard.

Gordy looked at the dozens of children. "Sarjo, are any of these yours?"

Sarjo smiled. "This is my village, so they are all mine. But am I their father? No. My son Abdoulie is 13. He is here. He works the fields with my wife and goes to school. You will meet him at dinner."

Sarjo opened the door. The two men carried their bags inside.

The room was small. No more than eight feet by six. Two narrow cots were pushed against the unpainted mud brick walls. The floors were dirt. But they had been swept clean. Gordy laughed to himself. How could dirt floors be clean? But they were. A simple wood table was pushed under the single window.

A door opened to the back. Stick fences separated their area from the units next door.

"No shower," sighed Gordy.

"Sure there is," Ross said, pointing to a large plastic pail. A gourd dipper hung above it on a nail. "Get undressed and stand on those flat rocks. I'll pour water over you. Then it's my turn."

After the two men had washed, Sarjo poked his head in the door. "The latrine is just outside the compound. Several compounds use it. And then we can go drop off the sugar with the alkallo."

Gordy hurried out the gate in the wall. He walked to the low screen of sticks Sarjo had identified as the latrine. Behind it was a six-foot shallow ditch. The strong smell of urine met him. He looked around. He was glad he had brought his package of tissues. Outside the latrine there was a pail of water warmed by the sun. Gordy washed his hands and returned to the compound.

Sarjo drove slowly through the village. He stopped under a tree. Across from them a large cement courtyard was surrounded by a compound in the shape of a "U." A metal-roofed porch ran around the inside. The roof was held up by crooked posts.

Sarjo unwired the trunk and pulled out the sugar. He led them into the courtyard. A group of several women and maybe 12 or 13 children sat under the roof on one side. "The alkallo's wives and children," Sarjo whispered. On the other side of the compound there was a raised platform. It had been made of bricks. There was a large wooden chair in the centre. An older man in a dark blue robe sat in the chair. The man had short white hair and a small white goatee that contrasted with his dark skin. He had a slight smile on his face. Gordy thought of ancient African kings.

Sarjo carried the bag to the platform. Two chairs were brought out for Ross and Gordy. They sat down facing the alkallo. Sarjo spoke for some time in Mandinka. Ross and Gordy heard their names several times. Finally Sarjo stopped. The alkallo spoke in a soft, low voice. He nodded to Gordy. Then he nodded to Ross. He spoke some more.

Sarjo turned to the two men. "He welcomes you to our village," he said. "He said he was especially pleased to have Canadians visit. They have done much for The Gambia." Sarjo paused. "And he extends a particular welcome to Ross. He called him our Mandinka cousin from far away."

Ross sat silent in his chair. He smiled at the alkallo. "Thank him for us," Ross said. "Tell him it is a great honour to be welcomed by him. Tell him it is very moving for me to come back to a Mandinka village."

Sarjo spoke some more. The alkallo's smile broadened. He nodded.

They got up and followed Sarjo to the car. He drove them back to his compound.

Sarjo parked in front of the brick wall. He turned around. "Would you like to walk around the village?"

Gordy felt the heat blast through the open windows. "Thanks, Sarjo, but I think I want to lie down for a while. Tomorrow maybe?"

"Certainly. And Mr. Ross?"

"I'd like that. Can Aime come?"

Sarjo smiled. "No. She is with her mother. Her friends. She would not walk with us."

Ross was disappointed. He shrugged. "OK. Let's go."

Gordy went into their room. Sarjo opened the back door of the Lada and let Ross out. They began walking through the dusty streets of the village.

Sarjo led Ross by the village well. It was surrounded by a circular cement brick wall. Women filled pails and plastic basins. They carried them back to their homes on their heads. Square mud brick houses lined the road. Most had thatched roofs. In the dirt yards, goats nibbled at a few shreds of grass. People walked by. "I sama," they said. "I be nyadi?" Sarjo chatted easily. Ross just smiled. Sarjo pointed out a huge baobob tree. It was leafless. It looked like it had been pulled from the earth and stuck back upside down. A stick fence surrounded it. "That's our cemetery," Sarjo said.

They walked by the alkallo's compound. People were crowded into the courtyard. Two men sat by a large purple plastic basin. It was filled with sugar. The men were giving it to villagers. They brought cans, cups and bowls.

"That is your sugar," Sarjo said. "We are very poor here. People cannot afford to buy sugar. The alkallo shares it among the community. Your gift was to the village."

Ross nodded. "So that's why you got such a big bag." He laughed. "I'll have to explain it to Gordy. He thought the chief was going to get diabetes."

They passed a raised stick platform under the shade of a tree. Men lay quietly on the surface in the suffocating heat. "That's called a bantaba," Sarjo said. "Men come here during the heat of the day. They talk and rest."

"Only men?" Ross asked.

"Only men."

"Sarjo," Ross said hesitantly as they walked. "I'm, I'm thinking of staying. Here. In The Gambia."

Sarjo kept walking. He acted like he had not heard. He pointed out dusty fields where farmers would be planting groundnuts soon. They walked by women watering vegetable gardens. He turned a corner. In front of them was a gigantic tree. It rose a hundred feet in the air. Its glossy green leaves shone in the sun. Sarjo led Ross under the tree. "This tree is 500 years old. That's what the griots tell us. People have always been taught under this tree. So when we built a school we built it here."

Ross followed Sarjo into a low building next to the tree. It was a simple rectangle of mud bricks with a metal roof. The hot metal roof had heated the interior like an oven. Ross felt the sweat roll down his face. His shirt clung to his back.

Low wooden benches were arranged in rows. The brick walls were once white. Now they were worn and chipped. A black rectangle had been painted on the brick at the front. "This is the blackboard," Sarjo said. "It doesn't work very well. But it doesn't really matter. There usually isn't any chalk anyway. This is the school where our children try to learn."

He walked out of the school and sat in the cool of the giant tree. Ross sat beside him. He leaned against the great trunk.

"What would you do?" Sarjo asked. "Here in The Gambia? You are not a rich man I think."

Ross sighed. "You're right there. I'm not a rich man. Maybe I could work in one of the hotels. I speak French and English." He sighed again. "I don't know."

Sarjo was silent for a long time. He closed his eyes. There was not the hint of a breeze. The heat was oppressive. Ross began to wonder if Sarjo had fallen asleep.

"We have a saying," Sarjo said at last. He did not open his eyes. "The millet plant soon wilts when pulled from the earth."

Sarjo stood up slowly. He began walking back to his compound. Ross stared after him for a moment. Then he got up and followed.

15

That evening Ross and Gordy sat in Sarjo's room. It was the same size as theirs. An old metal double bed filled one side of the small room. The mattress swayed deeply in the middle. A cover of bright blue and white batik cloth was spread over the bed. Gordy sat on the bed. Several low chairs were arranged around the room. Ross was on one. Sarjo's son Abdoulie and Sarjo's brother Ebrima sat on the other two. Sarjo sat on a wooden box.

Abdoulie spoke English well. He asked many questions about Canada. About the weather. About Vancouver. Were there really tall mountains in British Columbia? In The Gambia, Abdoulie told them, there were only a few hills. The tallest was 46 metres. Abdoulie laughed. "That is just 150 feet. In your country you have buildings higher than that, yes?"

The men spoke together. Ross looked around for Aime. He had not seen her all day. Juka brought in a large enamelled bowl. In it rice covered with chicken pieces in a deep red sauce steamed. She placed the bowl in the middle of the floor silently. Then Aime came through the door. She smiled shyly at the men. She gave

Ross and Gordy large metal spoons. Then she left through the front door.

Ross rose in his seat. "Won't Aime and Juka join us for dinner?"

Sarjo smiled. "Oh, no. The women eat by themselves."

Ross looked puzzled. "But why?"

Sarjo shrugged. "Why do the female and male lions hunt separately? Please, come eat. This is called benachin."

The Gambian men scooped up rice and sauce with the fingers of their right hand. Gordy hesitantly took a spoonful. It was spicy and delicious. There were peppers and onions in the dish. And slices of a small vegetable that looked like a wrinkled tomato.

Ross held up a piece on his spoon. "What is this?"

"Bitter tomato," Sarjo said. "You do not have this in Canada?"

Ross put his spoon into the mixture. Sarjo pulled meat off a chicken bone with his fingers. He placed it on Ross's spoon. Ross smiled to himself. Sarjo was trying to be polite. To make sure he got the best part of the chicken.

"Do you always eat like this?" Gordy asked, chewing a chicken wing.

Sarjo looked embarrassed. "For the past two weeks," Abdoulie said, "we have had only millet and milk. You brought the rice. We are celebrating your visit."

Gordy looked sheepish.

Ross did not see Aime again that night. And he only saw her briefly over the next two days of their stay. Sarjo visited friends and was gone much of the time. Abdoulie showed them around the community.

"There is not much here," he said apologetically. "We are a poor community."

"No," Ross said. "You do not have much materially. But you are rich in many ways."

Abdoulie smiled. "Perhaps. But there is little for young people to do. There is little future here. I want to get my education and go to Banjul. Like Aime. Maybe I could even come to Canada."

Ross grinned. "Maybe."

"It must be wonderful in Canada. Everyone is rich. Maybe you could help me go there?"

"Abdoulie," Ross said slowly. "I have a hard time making a living in Canada. Many people are poor. I mean, not like here..." How could he explain? "Many times I cannot find work. I have to pay a lot of money for rent. Food is very expensive. I have no family to go home to."

Abdoulie looked doubtful. "No family? How can that be?"

"My parents died. They lived far away. I rarely saw them. I have no other close relatives. The ones I do have I don't see or talk to much."

Abdoulie was silent. "You must be very lonely," he said.

The ride back to Banjul was quiet. Aime sat in the front seat. Ross seemed lost in thought. They pulled up in front of the Bungalow Beach as it was getting dark. Ross and Gordy gave Sarjo money for gas. They took their bags out of the trunk. Gordy started up to their room. He looked back at Ross. He was staring silently at Aime. She looked back at him.

Sarjo started the car and pulled away from the hotel.

That night Ross and Gordy sat on their veranda. The night was quiet and still. Only a faint cooling breeze blew in from the sea. They could smell the salt. The breeze was welcome after the unrelenting heat of the interior. There were two half-empty Julbrews on the plastic table.

Gordy broke the silence. "Our plane is leaving in two days."

Ross's face was lost in the shadows. "I know," he said softly.

"You, uh… You decided what you're going to do?"

Ross was quiet for a long time. Finally he spoke from the darkness.

"Sarjo told us two things. Do you remember the first saying? About the stump?"

"Oh yeah. And a crocodile or something."

" 'However long the stump of a tree has been in the river, it will never become a crocodile.' That's what he said."

"Yeah, I remember now."

"And then he said something to me in Manduar. 'The millet plant soon wilts when pulled from the earth.' "

Gordy sipped his beer. "Was he talking about you or Aime?"

"Both? Neither? Who knows?"

"So what are you going to do?" Gordy asked again.

"I'm having dinner tomorrow evening with Aime." His voice was quiet. Sad. "Give me till tomorrow night. OK?"

Gordy resisted an impulse to hug him. "Take as much time as you need, partner."

16

The ride out to the airport made the trip back from Manduar look like a parade. Ross and Aime sat in the back seat. Aime cried most of the way. Ross spoke to her softly. Gordy tried to make conversation with Sarjo. But for once Sarjo seemed silenced too. His usual smile was gone. His face was filled with pain and sorrow.

The route seemed almost familiar. Gordy remembered how odd and alien it had seemed just three weeks before. Then he had seen only dirt and poverty. Now he saw smiles and laughter. People who were content, connected, and part of a long history and strong culture. People struggling to make a living. Families walking to small white mosques. There was a pattern to it all. An ancient rhythm.

Inside shops, carpenters shaped chairs. A man in front of a tire shop banged a tire off its rim.

"Sarjo, you fixed that spare yet?"

Sarjo shrugged. But he smiled a little. "No time."

The airport was crazier than when they had arrived. Sarjo

pulled their luggage out of the trunk and carried it inside. A crush of people jammed around a single check-in booth. People were yelling and shoving. Sarjo spotted a porter he knew near the front. He yelled something in Mandinka. Then he passed their luggage over the heads of other passengers. He grabbed the tickets from Gordy and Ross and passed those to the man. Soon the porter returned with boarding passes and baggage slips.

Gordy pulled out 10 dalassis. He gave them to the man. "That saved us about two hours," he said to Ross.

But Ross was standing in a corner talking with Aime. Then he was holding her. Her shoulders shuddered. Ross pulled away. He walked toward Gordy. Gordy could see his eyes were filled with tears.

"Come on," he said hoarsely. "We'd better go."

Ross extended his right hand to Sarjo. But Sarjo shook his head. He held out his left hand. "In Gambia," he explained, "we shake goodbye with the left hand. This means we hope you will return some day." He took Ross's hand firmly. He looked into his eyes. "And who knows? Maybe you will."

Sarjo smiled and took Gordy's left hand. Then he went and stood by his daughter.

Ross stood a long minute staring at Aime. She managed one of her brilliant smiles for just one moment. Ross smiled back. He gave a little wave. He turned and headed through the security gate. Gordy looked one last time at Sarjo and Aime. Aime had her face buried in Sarjo's shoulder. Gordy turned and followed Ross.

Gordy found Ross sitting outside on the airport's veranda. He was sitting at a table drinking a Julbrew. Another one sat across from him. A black and white cat lay at his feet. Gordy sat down. He poured the beer into a glass.

"Any trouble getting through?" he asked.

"Nah." Ross didn't look at him.

"Ross, you sure this is what you want to do?"

Ross stared over the tarmac. Their red and white plane sat gleaming in the bright sunshine.

"What I want to do? I don't know. I don't know what I want."

"How'd you and Aime leave it?"

"We're going to stay in touch. You know, write and all. Who knows? Maybe she'll come visit me in Canada. Maybe I'll save up some money. Come back and open up a little beach bar." He gave a thin smile. "Make sure the African food is on time."

"A beach bar? Over here?"

"Sure. Why not?"

"Well, you know. All that crocodiles and rivers stuff."

Ross was quiet for a moment. "Rivers are powerful, you know. They can do pretty amazing things." He reached down to pet the cat. She purred and arched against his hand. "Who knows? Maybe a stump can change into a crocodile. It wouldn't be easy. But over time. And with a lot of work."

Gordy grinned. "At least you've got the advantage of *looking* like a crocodile."

"Yeah, well. Right now I don't feel much like one."

The loudspeaker crackled announcing their flight. Other passengers began to move toward the plane.

Ross stood up and put his bag over his shoulder. He looked at Gordy. "Come on, partner," he said. "Let's go home."